AB166

THE WEATHER
CHANGED, SUMMER
CAME
AND SO ON

THE WEATHER CHANGED, SUMMER CAME AND SO ON

PEDRO CARMONA-ALVAREZ

Translated by Diane Oatley

LONDON NEW YORK CALCUTTA

Seagull Books, 2015

First published as *Og været skiftet og det ble sommer og så videre*
by Pedro Carmona-Alvarez
© Kolon Forlag 2012

English translation © Diane Oatley, 2015

This translation has been published with the financial support of NORLA

ISBN   978 0 8574 2 236 1

British Library Cataloguing-in-Publication Data
A catalogue record for this book is available from the British Library

Typeset by Seagull Books, Calcutta, India
Printed and bound by Maple Press, York, Pennsylvania, USA

PART ONE

My dad said I had to sleep in the living room, they didn't have a guest room, he and Tina, so I had to sleep on a cot that Tina called the Mule because it was so uncomfortable. I didn't think so. I'd just turned 17. I could have slept right on the floor. I was used to just about everything; when the parties in Bergen ended, I could sleep anywhere.

I remember California. I remember the afternoon light and the view from the house, all misty and strange. Dad took me for drives. We would stand and look at the ocean. He said that was part of what he liked best about getting older, that you did things that before you would have just dismissed with a sneer. He said watching the waves did him good, to think about what they were trying to say. He wanted to show me Mision Viejo. Tina came along. Nothing here, Dad said. We moved on to

3

San Diego, but when we arrived it was dark, eighty thousand lights switched off. We drove through the streets, ate hamburgers in the car. I saw a whole lot of night-kids, under-the-bridge-kids. And girls like me. Skinny girls in Converse sneakers. Girls who trembled, pulled down their jeans and thought about their souls all afternoon long.

I took pictures all the time. The living room faced the bay and the ridge full of houses and buildings. Dad talked about Tina and asked about Mum. I would stand and stare at the sea. Do you like the house? he asked. Tina took me to a garage sale. One day we called Dad and said he had to come pick us up because Tina had bought a merry-go-round horse and a porcelain cow that she wanted to put out on the porch. She showed me a collection of seashells, a papier-mâché horse she'd made herself and two wooden angel heads. I liked Tina. She looked at my pictures when I'd had them developed, asked if she could keep some of them. When I went home, she'd covered a shoebox in velvet, inside she put three Mexican ceramic devils, as a gift. Two of them had insect bodies, the third looked like a butterfly.

The dining room was narrow, with an almost invisible door at the end. A winding staircase wormed upwards to their bedroom. Tina usually went to bed early and Dad and I would sit and talk. He asked me about Mum, about Bergen. We smoked cigarettes and drank beer. He put on records I hadn't heard before, records I brought with me when I went home again, that Johannes and Andreas and the others recorded on tapes that we listened to until they fell apart. You've gotta hear this one, he said. He went to get beer from the fridge. We hardly talked about the accident. He asked about Mum and I had to tell him. Sometimes when she couldn't sleep, Tina came down to join us. She asked about Mum and then I'd talk about Mum and about the guy from Bergen and about myself.

One evening Dad asked me if I blamed him. I said no.

But I left, he said.

Yeah, I said. You left.

But you're not angry with me, Marita?

No, I said, You were so skinny.

I remember California. Then I flew to New York and visited Grandma Dixie before I went home at the end of the summer. To Bergen and to Mum and to my friends. Johannes, whom I'd hardly thought about. And Andreas. And the others. And then we went back to being who we'd been before the holidays. The same ones as in the spring and winter and autumn before, the same ones who pushed the rest of the summer forward, wary of all of the straight kids at school and the church and the church's power and the right wing, before we remembered, all of a sudden, that we were just kids and simple and that the only thing we knew how to do was to be awake and sleep with one another like crazy.

We're like shadows, I said to Dad as we stood and watched the waves. I'd told him what kind of girl I was. I had to tell him the truth, that we were like shadows creeping across Torgalmenningen Square, through Friday nights and fist fights and the 80s.

Dad lived in Norway from 1967. In Oslo, in Bekkelaget. He and Mum came here after the accident, after my sisters had died over there in the States. That was before I was born. It's strange how childhood always seems completely normal until you grow up and start talking to other grown-ups about childhood. That's when you discover things. All the strange things. Only then do you see things clearly, and realize that you always saw them clearly.

Right?

You understand such things, right?

*

Liv was Mum's friend. She isn't important but I had to start calling Mum Kari and that was always when Liv was around. After Dad left and the guy from Bergen showed up and Mum bought all those new clothes and, afterwards, when the guy from Bergen didn't come and Mum started bringing men home with her and told me to call her Kari.

Sometimes Liv brought her daughter too, whom I didn't like and whom I once bit until she bled, and Mum went crazy but not as crazy as Liv. Then I tried to bite Liv too, but Mum got hold of my hair and pulled it so hard that she ended up with a huge tuft of hair in her fist. Afterwards she cried and called me her little doll and her breath always smelt from then on.

It was during that time. When we were still living in Bekkelaget. When the guy from Bergen started coming and when he didn't show up, there were other men. But the guy from Bergen was the only one for Kari. She said so later, long after we'd arrived on the train to Bergen. We'd been living in the little house for many years and the Bergen guy had almost stopped coming, but not quite.

He makes me dotty, she said.

She used the word dotty. It wasn't a common word for these parts.

He was all right I guess. He smelt too, but not the way the others smelt. I tried to dislike him.

Maybe I tried to blame everything on the guy from Bergen, but it didn't work. Dad was still writing me letters then, and in one of them he said that I mustn't be unfair. That Mum deserved to be happy.

And she was happy. At least for a while. She blamed Dad and said ugly things about him but she was happy. She put on make-up, and Liv came to visit and once in a while she brought her daughter, but not so often after I bit her.

I was 12, almost 13. Dad was the one who moved out. One day he woke up, opened the closet and threw trousers and shirts into a blue bag before coming into my room and trying to explain things that almost couldn't be explained. Then he was gone, but he was still nearby. In Bjølsen, at Marty's place. He called me. I met him at the National Theatre station, outside. I met him at the square Youngstorget, and outside the department store Glasmagasinet. We went to Kaffistova. Dad had coffee and I got to eat whatever I wanted, which wasn't much.

He was the one who took off and it was his fault things turned out the way they did. At least that's what Kari said for the rest of what little childhood I had left, before adolescence got its fangs into me. But that's later, in Bergen, in Nordnes, in a little wooden house in an alleyway.

Later other things will happen. To Kari. To me.

And they will happen in a kind of haze.

But first I have to grow up.

Then my grandfather died, and my dad went home. He wrote to me, said he couldn't stand being in New Jersey anymore, and then he left for LA and sent letters from different places on the West Coast. He was looking for a place to stay while I was growing up in Bergen. Afternoons and mornings of light rain, but also the kind of rain that splashed and splashed for days on end. Heavy rain. The kind of rain that howled and the whole town ended up looking like a wet and dripping cellar. The streets of Bergen—C. Sundts gate, up along Tollbodallmenningen and Strandgaten, past Nagelgården towards the park. My room at Nordnes, our house, where everything smelt of dust and leather. The wind that would tousle my hair and the trees, restless, back and forth like nervous kids in the Bergen rain.

Later I grow up, and the nights fill up with knees and hands, nights with something almost electric in the bones of my face. Nights when I am luminescent, as if made of plastic.

Later I open my mouth, sometimes to kiss, sometimes to snap and sometimes to talk about Johnny Richards and all that.

Then Dad left. It was a few months after he'd taken me to the Drammen Concert Hall to see Bruce Springsteen. We talked about it, that he was going to leave. I'll give him that. He let me know. When he moved out. When my grandfather died and he had to leave. He always answered me. He did the best he could, I saw that. He was so thin and gristly and he tried not to seem sad. He said everything was going to be fine. He left me his record player, his records. After he'd gone to the US, before Mum and I moved to Bergen, I sat in his office, curled up in his chair, and listened to Bruce Springsteen like crazy, and I cried and cried like the kid I was.

He said he'd write and he did for a while. Later the letters tapered off, but it didn't matter. Mum always tried to vilify him because of it. He doesn't even write to his own daughter, she said, as if *she* behaved like a saint.

But that wasn't how it was, it wasn't how it worked between me and him. I've always known the difference between important and unimportant things. What matters and what's just bullshit. And then we moved to Bergen and Mum was happy for a little while and I liked the stillness of school. I always liked living in Bergen. And then Kari started shaking and you know the rest.

But a lot of stuff happens before that.

1956

They arrived in New York at the end of November, having travelled on the America Line from Stockholm. There was a peaceful snowfall, Kari thought it looked like play-snow, and as they drove through the streets she imagined somebody sitting in a corner of the city, cutting up pieces of paper and throwing them over the buildings with huge fists. During those first days she felt as if the ground was rocking beneath her, like on the ship, and she wondered whether Manhattan moved like that because it was an island. That the city seemed like a labyrinth was something she didn't think about till later, when she began going out on her own, taking Ylva with her. First they just walked around the block. A few days later, down three blocks and then up again. Then they ventured over to the duck pond and back. The next day they went down four blocks, two to the left and home again the same way. Ylva said it was like Hansel and Gretel and the white pebbles they dropped behind them in the woods.

Yeah, except we have neither pebbles nor crumbs, Kari said. She tried to pay attention, to remember where things were in relation to the park, the library or

11

other large buildings. But just when she was certain about where she and her sister were, a building would suddenly pop up on the opposite side from where it'd been the day before, the traffic ran in the opposite direction and the streets and traffic lights and skyscrapers seemed to move, to change places, disappear and reappear anywhere. That was when she thought of the labyrinth, but it was a strange word.

To her sister she said: Yeah, a forest.

The apartment was on Park Avenue and it was huge, old-fashioned and modern at the same time, with dark, heavy furniture and light, transparent curtains. Sigurd worked for the Norwegian Foreign Ministry's trade division. Synnøve was supposed to keep house and take care of the girls, who would start school at Brearly in the New Year—a private school for girls on 83rd Street. Kari quickly made friends there. Neat, well-dressed girls who invited her home, to apartments that resembled their apartment, where the living rooms looked like their living room; in the girls' homes, too, the dining-room tables were massive and dark, chandeliers hung from the ceilings and there were spacious offices into which the fathers would retire after meals.

They belonged to the same world.

In Norway they'd also belonged to a sort of upper class, but here it was different. Her friends were well dressed and their conversation well bred. When they were alone, they often imitated the adult world. It was a kind of game, and at the same time it was not. The fathers were politicians, diplomats, lawyers, doctors. The mothers organized social gatherings and dinners. On Saturdays, the families strolled leisurely through Central Park and the afternoons ended in the big department stores on 5th Avenue, where the mothers floated around like ballerinas, like women on a stage.

Kari had to adapt, imitate.

Johnny had been thrown out of the private university in Lakewood. For a long time he'd been harassed by one of the deans, a huge Italian with turtle-like hands. Johnny didn't understand why the dean disliked him so intensely, he'd tried to ignore it all, thinking maybe that would help. He was not a bad student. Not a model student either, but he could hardly be called a trouble-maker. He'd been disciplined on a few occasions, there had been a few episodes, but to Johnny it seemed as if the Italian had decided to focus all of his hostility on him. He'd put up with it, tried to ignore the sarcasm and the rude remarks, but in the end it had been too much. When he was called into the dean's office for something he hadn't done—somebody had stuffed a bunch of bananas into the exhaust pipe of a car belonging to one of the teachers—Johnny made it clear that he would no longer put up with such abuse. It doesn't make any difference that you're a rich man's boy here, Richards, the dean had said. Your father has no power in here, you know. I'm the one in charge here. *Oh, what a kingdom*, Johnny said, before the turtle-like hand hit him in the face with a brutal force. Johnny felt the tears flowing, the kind of tears you shed when you're a child and can't do anything but weep. That was when Johnny kicked the dean in the groin. And the Italian crumpled, clutching his scrotum as he turned white and dropped to his knees. He looked like a kind of saint, Johnny thought, as his eyes looked up towards the ceiling, like one of those paintings of Christian martyrs.

Johnny was expelled the same day. When Paul found out, he was furious. At home he talked to his son about shame and decency and responsibility. Johnny tried to respond but Paul refused to listen. It's no good making excuses, he said.

But you're not listening, Johnny said.

I don't need to listen, the father said. I know.

No, you don't, Johnny said and left.

He took a few things with him and went over to Billy's house, where he slept in one of the guest rooms.

A week passed.

Dixie was worried sick. The house was so quiet and empty and she had nightmares that her son was dead, that he'd drowned or been run over or stabbed.

14

One day, on his way to work, Paul spotted Johnny. He was sitting on the bonnet of a car with a girl. Paul turned the car around, drove home and told Dixie, who got into the car right away and in a moving scene on the street managed to convince Johnny to come home again.

A few weeks passed.

Father and son circled each other. Paul thought Johnny should grow up more quickly, I don't know what it is about this generation, he said.

Dixie said it'd be OK, he would come around, remember yourself at his age.

She kept them in their respective corners.

Life. The spring of 1957. Driving his father's car down to Billy's place, to talk about girls who willingly unzip their jeans in the back seats of cars, secretly, in toilet stalls, in some hole or other where the beer is cheap, the food greasy and the pool tables slanted and shabby.

Sleeping late, climbing over fences at night, with Billy, with Luke and The Doctor. Sitting still, leaning against a tree until it gets light and that strange blue light appears at the far edges of the sky. Eyes shiny and ready at daybreak. Being eighteen years old. Being nineteen years old, empty hands, see-through hands, hands that can climb anything. Booze like water. Roast chickens and twisted forks. Billy's record player spinning like the earth, the used razor blades, the TV sets that are carried into the house, a tiny statue trembling on a bookshelf, a childhood that keeps disappearing, a tennis player coated with fool's gold, just about to serve.

Life. The spring of 1957.

Every minute is a plastic trophy.

Dixie kept them in their respective corners, and Paul finally offered his son a job at the textile factory. His father had approached him slowly, as if on padded feet.

Johnny sat down and listened to him.

Paul talked about the time before the war, about the South Bronx and Johnny's birth. Before Pearl Harbor, when the economy was still a mess.

Things got better. Calmer.

Dixie tousled their hair, one after the other, as they walked past her where she stood holding their lunch boxes, ready to wave them off from the stairs in the morning.

Kari is out walking in the park with her friend Joyce and Joyce's brother Philip, a boy with hips like a girl, who's been buzzing around Kari like a gadfly for weeks. They've been to the pictures and seen a film that Philip chose; a film about the future, a film full of creatures from outer space, men and women wearing helmets and shiny overalls. The two girls have been whispering and giggling for the better part of the film. Philip—who is two, almost three years older than the girls—has been certain that his age is his strongest card, up to now. But when he scolds his sister on the way out of the film, and his sudden authoritative tone makes her friend giggle even more, he gets sullen and nervous. He doesn't know what he should do or say. The girls feel guilty, they're just laughing at a girl, they say, someone at school, someone he doesn't know. Philip's not sure he can trust them, but when Kari asks if they can walk home through the park, when Kari walks between the siblings and holds each of them by the arm, when she even assures Philip that she loved the film he'd chosen, then something releases in his face; he can feel Kari's arm against his own and sees her smile at him, but when he asks about what the girl they'd been laughing at had done, Kari lays her head on his shoulder and says: Oh we can't tell you that, unfortunately.

You know.

Girl stuff.

Johnny sits on a bench in Central Park, with Luke and Billy. They smoke cigarettes and talk about what kind of cars they dream of, which cars they'll buy one day, what kind of rims they want and what colour leather seats. Cadillac. Buick. Chevrolet. Studebaker. Billy says he likes European cars too. Aston Martin, he says, but Luke and Johnny start booing, whistling. You can't be serious. Not if you've seen the new Chrysler.

They're waiting for a film to begin.

They comb their hair with their hands.

They kill time.

Kari and her friend are sitting on a bench a short distance away. Philip gets in line to buy ice cream. It's a warm day, the line is endless over by the ice-cream man, and the boys strike up a conversation with the girls because or because or because. Neither Kari nor Johnny will remember it later, in the future that will come; neither of them will remember how it started, but they will remember other things—Kari will picture Johnny freshly shaven, and remind him that he was the first to introduce himself, and he didn't look at her friend at all. Johnny will remember the squirrel that looked down at them from a tree, the sounds from a playground nearby and Kari's lovely, bare legs, how she crossed them while she was eating her ice cream, looking at him.

They're waiting for the film to start, the boys, and meanwhile we're sitting here, on this faithful bench of ours, Johnny says.

They wait.

Another film?

No, the same film.

The one about the future.

A coincidence.

Kari and Joyce want to stay, but Philip understands everything, why the boys suddenly become sarcastic with him and why the girls giggle at their taunts. He hurries to finish his ice cream, gets to his feet and becomes all grown-up and serious. He tries to look Kari in the eye. But his gaze doesn't reach her, neither does his voice when he speaks. All this helpless character is now capable of doing is to provide shade from the sun, because Kari and Johnny have already seen each other, their gazes are just as inexplicable as they are obvious, just as self-assured as they are nervous, shy and inquisitive.

Kari says she's staying.

And Philip—who paid for the film ticket, who for weeks now has been going for walks with Kari in the park, yes, Kari who even let his hand rest on her own during a rowing trip the previous weekend (and she hadn't removed it!)—he doesn't understand a thing. He doesn't know what he's done wrong. He has believed so many things, and when he and his sister walk away, he finds himself in the midst of a mystery that, to him, is as big as the universe.

Beautiful accent, Johnny says when the siblings have left. Where are you from?

The sky is as light blue as a jumper.

His friends say they have to go if they're going to catch the film, but it's as if the voices are drenched in reverb, as if Billy were miles away and Johnny could barely hear him.

Kari is 17 years old.

Her lightness is striking. A cloud of the self-evident surrounds her.

That's how beauty manifests itself—shy, as if surprised.

And all things that sparkle.

Her eyes and his eyes when finally they are alone, when they get up and Kari straightens her dress and starts walking and they see each other's shadows in front of them, also glittering, mercurial beneath the sky, a light blue jumper pulled down over New York, over the park's winding paths, over the romantic bridges they amble across, past an ancient tree, crooked and bending over: As if it's falling, Johnny says, and hasn't yet hit the ground.

Something's burning in their guts.

Something that makes Kari laugh too hard when he says something, and something that makes Johnny laugh too hard when she answers.

Do you like climbing trees, I mean, did you like it when you were a kid?

Oh yes.

Oh yes.

Oh yes.

They get married in New York. August 1958. They still have those round youthful faces, the kind of eyes that are sparkling with dreams. They rent a house in Free-hold, not far away from Paul and Dixie, a house that creaks at night, a little old house they both love living in, even though it's draughty, even though they must bundle up in quilts when they eat in the wintertime. But Kari makes it nice. She buys tablecloths, carpets, glass figurines that she puts on a sideboard that Paul brings in one day. At night they barely sleep. They smoke cigarettes and look at the ceiling and tell each other everything, all kinds of things.

Kari talks about the war, her father's war, stories she's heard from her mother; about the Germans who marched into Norway, about her father and mother on the island of Hiskjo, outside Bømlo county, where an uncle took them in. About the fishing boat that trans-ported dissidents to the little island of Møkster in Austevoll, and about Milorg, the underground organi-zation that helped them get out of the country. Johnny smokes and listens. He listens to the names. To the strange words that Kari pronounces with some other kind of mouth, as if the words came from another place than when she otherwise spoke. She tells him about the partisan bases in the mountains and forests all around the country and Johnny tries to envision the landscape, the trees, the knolls and cottages made of stone. The Bokna Fjord and the Sands Fjord. Suldal in Rogaland and the southern side of the Bømla Fjord. Hardanger and Eidfjord. Bergen. Johnny's parents have given them a radio, almost the same as the one Dixie has at their place, a huge cabinet with a record player. At night Johnny puts on the records that filled up his childhood. Dixie's records. From the most traditional big-band jazz to progressive be-bop. As often as she can, Mum goes to jazz concerts, he says. Once a month she dresses up and forces Dad to go with her in to Manhattan to hear live music. But Dad doesn't like it. He thinks they're too old for that kind of thing. He's a little scared of black people, too. Johnny lies there and holds Kari in his arms. She says she's cold. He says he loves this record and Kari laughs at him and says it's just noise. He gets to his feet, pretending to be offended, and tells her about the time Elvis appeared on Ed Sullivan, even then, Johnny says after they've slept together, even when Elvis twisted his hips and the girls swooned like flies— no, nothing compared to Bird.

Kari laughs at him.

It's a good laughter. A laughter that fills up the little room, that fills up the darkness, white teeth, tiny moons dangling in front of his face. She turns up the volume. She prefers Paul Anka and Neil Sedaka and Rickie Valens and Pat Boone.

And Elvis, but mostly when he does slow songs.

I'm a simple girl, Kari says.

Sometimes it feels as if they're playing house. He comes home from the textile factory, she's made dinner and even though he is only two years older, he thinks she looks so young. She's bought new clothes. She's trying to look like a woman. He lets her decide which radio stations they listen to; it's no sacrifice for him to listen to sugary-sweet music or smarmy ballads. Johnny believes it's possible to love everything she loves. That's how love works, he thinks. They joke about how different they are. You can't compare *Rickie Sings Again* to *Sketches of Spain*, you just can't, Johnny says, but Kari answers that she can't understand what he gets out of all that noise he likes; it's especially awful when Johnny plays John Coltrane or Ornette Coleman, then she puts her hands over her ears and later, in the future that will come, she will also put her hands over the girls' ears and laugh a laughter not to be found in Oslo, a laughter that will stay behind in a grave resembling a garden in New Jersey.

One night, Kari says that when she was younger she was afraid Ylva would turn out to be prettier than her, and Johnny goes quiet and turns on the light on the night table and says that nobody is more beautiful than she is. Nobody. He tells her the stories he knows—the one about California and that long summer he spent there with Billy's parents; about the time Dixie dressed him up in one of his father's suits, combed his hair and put a tie on him, so he could get into Birdland to see Charlie Parker with her, but also stories he's never told before; during the nights Kari learns that Paul and Dixie came to the US as children, from Odessa, he tells her the little he knows about why Dixie broke off contact with her family, he says he barely remembers his grandfather and that his grandmother died before he was born.

When Kari gets pregnant, the grandparents-to-be race out to buy as much as possible for the baby. The little house in Freehold is filled up with two sets of everything, pink in case it's a girl and blue if it's a boy.

Vera is born on 21 October 1959, the same day that the corkscrew-shaped Guggenheim Museum opens in New York. While the birth is underway, Paul, Sigurd and Johnny sit in a bar close to the hospital. They talk in fits and starts. They smoke like demons, all three of them. Johnny is nervous, but wants to appear indifferent. He drinks quickly. They don't talk about the birth. They talk about how much the museum costs, about whether spending so much money on a building can be justified, regardless of who's paying for it. Paul orders food. Sigurd jokes that the child will most likely be an artist, being born on such a day.

God forbid, Paul says.

Johnny cries and cries when he takes Vera in his arms. His mouth smells of whisky and cigarettes. The gigantic knot he's had in his stomach during the past weeks is gone, as if it evaporated, inside him a light is shining; he takes the child in his arms, he lifts her as carefully as he can, terrified that she will break, like a vase, like a porcelain figurine, like something at once infinitely beautiful and fragile. Kari lies in the hospital bed and watches him with tired eyes, shining like a thousand suns, like the finest of all stars. I love you, he says, and gives in to tears sweeter than anything he's ever known. The tiny heart beating against the palm of his hand. The tiniest heart. The biggest thing he's ever felt.

Synnøve has prepared Kari's old room on Park Avenue. That's where she convalesces after the birth, while she learns to talk to the little one in a voice she didn't realize she had. Johnny takes time off from work for a few days, even though Paul doesn't give his consent. He stays in the guest room and can't sleep. He looks out the window. He sneaks in to watch Kari and Vera who are sleeping side by side. He tries to tiptoe out and the little one wakes up and wails and he says he doesn't mind rocking her. He, too, has a new voice, another man's voice. A father's voice.

It's decided that the families will celebrate Christmas Eve together at Synnøve and Sigurd's place. It's the first time the presents will be opened on Christmas Day and not on Christmas Eve the way they do in Norway. Dixie decides that they're going to have turkey for dinner and for Synnøve that comes out of nowhere; all day long she stands there in the kitchen with Dixie, reduced to some kind of assistant in her own home. But it's delicious, they all agree about that. Ylva asks if they can have turkey next year as well, and Sigurd says they would have to wait and see about that. So they talk about food. Synnøve and Dixie talk about traditional Norwegian Christmas fare—mutton and potato dumplings and pork loin. It's sort of expected that they will converse, but they don't quite manage to hit it off. Synnøve thinks that Dixie is often too strong-willed, that she has too many opinions about all sorts of things that Synnøve couldn't care less about. Besides, her stories are never-ending. She goes on and on, even when Synnøve has started glancing away, hinting that the monologues have gone on long enough.

But the fathers get on well.

They each see in the other a co-conspirator, but also an opponent. When they talk about the economy, about political issues, there is an underlying power struggle, so subtle, so well hidden that only their spouses sense it. They always listen to each other attentively. Both are curious about the other's knowledge, but it happens that they get hung up on details and things of little importance. When this happens, it doesn't take long, nonetheless, before one of them admits to being wrong, whereupon the other quickly makes it clear how insignificant the whole matter was.

The easiest thing is to talk about the little girl.

That's always easy.

Vera lies in a cradle by the Christmas tree. When she wakes up, she is lifted up by each of them, one after the other, the huge dark eyes examine everything, sometimes she makes noises, throws out her arms and drools from her little toothless mouth. After they have had coffee and eaten Christmas cookies (the traditional seven different kinds, baked by Synnøve and Ylva), Paul and Sigurd get to their feet at the same time, say they would like to make a toast to the grandchild, to Kari and to Johnny and to the future, before they ceremoniously announce that the families have come to a mutual decision that the young married couple's future lies in Asbury Park, where the textile factory's new branch will be up and running in the course of the coming year.

A house of their own, in Asbury Park.

THE WEATHER CHANGED

And the textile factory.

That's the future.

They move out of the house in Freehold right after New Year's in 1960. Johnny goes to work wearing dark, tailor-made suits. Twenty-two years old, he is a youngster in the eyes of the newly hired employees, a spoilt kid born with a silver spoon in his mouth, but as the months pass, that's also the only objection they have to him; as a boss, he is neither visible nor formidable, most of them would say he's absent, even though his office—well-lit and modern, enclosed by acoustic glass—looms over the entire factory. The employees nod politely when, on the rare occasion, he comes down to make an inspection. They call him Mr Richards and so does Walter Rosenberg, who has just turned forty, who makes important decisions all the time but lets Johnny think that he is the one responsible for them. Rosenberg who had to let a whole year pass before coming to terms with the bitterness that swelled up inside him when Paul Richards put the whippersnapper in charge of running the textile factory's new branch and not Rosenberg himself, as many had expected, yes, even counted on.

When Johnny has finished for the day, he drives home to Kari and Vera in a brand-new Chevrolet Impala Sedan. Hardtop. Panoramic rear window. He throws his suit jacket onto the back seat, folds up his shirt sleeves and rolls down the window. At home, dinner awaits him and almost every day he finds something new in the house; Kari buys plants, tablecloths, decorates the living room with lamps and an elegant but, honestly, too-expensive living-room set she saw photos of in a women's magazine that both Dixie and Synnøve recommended. They can afford to splurge a bit. They deserve it. He kisses her on the forehead and shakes his head as if Kari is a child who has done something cute. After dinner he lies down on the couch to rest. At night Kari gets up, makes sure Vera is asleep and doesn't make any noise because Johnny must be rested when he goes off to work.

Daddy has to sleep.

Ann is born the next summer. The new baby, a moon-dancer, her eyes open, almost black, the tiny hands grasping at the air, around his fingers, squeezing and hanging on tight to her father. The summer's so hot that nobody can sleep, not Johnny, not Kari and not the girls. It's a sleepless summer, but it doesn't matter. Kari lifts up the baby even though her arms are about to buckle, even though the fatigue is like a kind of bear releasing all of its weight upon her. Then it grows cooler and the birds down by the seaside hang and soar

31

suspended on the air currents. Kari goes out to the porch and cools off with a Coke, with Paul's lemonade, with handkerchiefs full of ice cubes from the new refrigerator.

On Park Avenue the girls can run and jump as much as they want. Kari and Ylva look at each other in disbelief when Vera and Ann dance on the coffee table, when Sigurd talks to them in a voice he never used with either of them back when they were little. But Kari likes it. She likes that her parents have become softer, in a way, that the girls, because they're just kids, also make them child-like; Sigurd on all fours, grandfather like a horse, grandmother clapping her hands when the girls want to stand up on the good chairs in the living room and sing for her. Johnny in the background. They speak to each other in Norwegian when they forget, when they don't notice Johnny standing in the doorway.

He takes it as a good sign.

He and Kari take the lift down to the lobby. They take the lift and hold hands. New York is cold and yellow, they cross the streets, the cars are almost motionless, everything is as if under water. Yellow-red leaves on the pavement, all over the lawns. The entire city dancing a dance only they can see; a gust of wind, hands lifting in greeting, birds and cars look the same on the outskirts of their gaze—the blue sky of happiness, chalk hearts melting into each other on a stone wall. They walk slowly. Sometimes they go to the cinema, sometimes they buy more things for the house or sit down on a bench and talk about the girls. That's how it is with the girls; regardless of how much there is to talk about otherwise—the house, their parents, the factory—they always return to Vera and Ann.

Did you see her last night? one of them says. Did you see her when she stumbled and turned around and looked for us before she started to cry?

Ann has your eyes, the other one says. I'm so glad. And I'm glad Vera is not jealous either, you know, that she looks after her sister. Did you see what happened on the beach when your parents came to visit that Sunday?

Yeah. I know. She's fantastic.

Both of them.

Yeah, both of them.

And us. We are lucky.

You bet we are.

*

Synnøve helps Kari with the house and the children when Sigurd is out on long business trips. Kari prepares the guest room, there is something satisfying about welcoming her mother in her own home. Doing simple things, putting new sheets on the bed, taking out towels.

It's almost as if they have become reacquainted, Kari says to Johnny one evening, or at least acquainted in another way. Ylva laughs at her sister and mother, says they are like two old biddies. But they wave it away, Ylva will understand all of this later on, when she gets older, when she too has a child and a husband and a house. Both mother and daughter are proud of themselves; they like this new way of spending time together, as if they have become girlfriends, almost.

Do you think I look like my mum? Kari says one evening when her mother is visiting. She and Johnny are sitting in the living room. Synnøve has gone to bed early and the girls are asleep.

No, Johnny says.

Are you sure?

Yes, he says.

I don't believe you, she says, and they start laughing, and Johnny says that he is exactly like Paul sometimes, that he sees it himself, and there is nothing that irritates him more.

And your mother, Kari says. Always bringing us things. Bringing *me* things. For the house.

She's just trying to be nice, Johnny says.

I know, she says. My mum's the same way. With all her gifts.

God, they're so old-fashioned sometimes, Johnny says.

I know, Kari says. Then she gets up and turns on the radio. The volume turned down low, so the girls won't wake up.

And speaking of old-fashioned, she says. I've been thinking, perhaps we should buy a new radio.

I like this radio, Johnny says, a little surprised.

But it takes up so much space, Kari says.

We have enough room.

Kari wrinkles her nose. But it's so 1950s, she says.

And that's how it is—the preceding decade seems so remote from the new, from the America that is now America, the young, hopeful America that exists before somebody blows John F. Kennedy's head off and everything starts to grow dark.

When the Soviets deploy missiles in Cuba, they all hold their breath. Johnny says everything will be fine but he knows that's just a lie and Kari knows it too. Daily life fills up with cargo ships transporting missiles, moving across the afternoons like snapping wolves. At the office, Johnny sits and reads the newspapers while he thinks about Kari and the girls. He gets up and looks out across the production hall. The words, like towers—blockade, defence doctrine. Maybe now it's going to happen. He holds Kari for a long time, standing in the middle of the living room, with a fear that feels like hunger, a hunger he must hide. They have seen the images from Hiroshima and Nagasaki on television, maybe that's how it will be. Many days and many nights go by and everything is illuminated by fear, a white, blinding anxiety about what could happen to Kari, to the girls, to all of them, dreams so white that Johnny wakes up terror-stricken and wondering if he hears rumbling, and if the rumbling is the beginning of the end and how it would feel to be burnt alive.

But it all turns out fine. It passes.

They say so on TV.

The family gathers in Freehold, at Dixie and Paul's. They get together in Asbury Park. Kari, Johnny and the girls go into Manhattan. They say almost nothing, because there is almost nothing to be said.

They hug one another.

And life, life feels like a gift.

In the aftermath of the fear—in a kind intoxicated state—Johnny decides to invest in a project that cousin Howard has had going for a while. Howard is Aunt Zoe's eldest child, a small, stoutly built and long-nosed man, three, almost four years older than Johnny. Just a few days before Christmas Eve in 1962, Johnny and Howard buy two old buildings in Ocean Grove, which they renovate over the course of the winter. The plan is to rent them out to tourists in the summer season. Paul is sceptical, for him earning money is associated with work, with producing something, with offering people a service at least. Food. Coffee. Clothing. Finally he goes along with lending Johnny money, but makes it clear that Johnny is borrowing the money and that Ocean Grove is not to distract him from the work at the factory.

The family business should come first, his father says.

Always.

And Johnny says he agrees, in a way.

1963: The summer photographs show a happy little family. The Fourth of July. The girls wearing yellow dresses, Johnny like a Marlon Brando in a white T-shirt and big black shoes with a Coke in one hand and an American flag in the other. His friends came to visit on Sundays, alone or with their wives, girlfriends, fiancées who compliment Kari on the house and the girls and the interior decoration. The men talk about the Major League games and pop open can after can of beer. Ylva loves coming out to Asbury Park to visit, she loves the girls and she loves the beach and for a while she even believes that she is in love with Johnny; Ylva who will turn 16 in America, 17 in America, 18 years old, who celebrates her 18th birthday in Asbury Park, by the ocean, in a picture taken by the ocean, wearing a lovely green dress, with her niece on her lap.

The summer is photographed using the new camera, the summer and 20 or so photos which later, in the future that will come, will try to cheat death. The water that laps over the girls' feet and Kari who lifts Ann up by her arms while the little girl smiles and gurgles out things nobody understands.

Vera who talks to everyone.

Says thank you and please.

Twenty or so photos depicting the unbearable— Johnny and Kari so in love with each other, with the life they are living. Johnny Richards, his blonde wife and the overwhelming feeling of success that they emanate. Everything that their parents see. Their friends. Their neighbours. All those who catch a glimpse of Johnny down at Ocean Grove when he's holding Kari's hand, on the way into a tiny restaurant where they order pasta and red wine, Coca Cola for the little ones.

Johnny and Kari in the grips of an unfathomable happiness, an almost unheard of kind of amorous good fortune.

They don't know how beautiful they are.

That is the core of their shared beauty.

The photographs.

Twenty or so photographs.

Johnny and Kari and the girls. Like seeing a falling star.

After having rented out the apartments to rich southerners all summer, Johnny and Howard find out that the bank has no misgivings about lending them money for another two buildings—one on Kingsley Street, the other right by the restaurant Mrs Jays, which will later be turned into The Stone Pony and play a significant part in the young Bruce Springsteen's life. Johnny goes around in work clothes almost the entire autumn. He wants to take part. He is building himself, watching as he comes into his own. He likes to tear down walls, he likes carpentry, in the evenings he shows Kari the blue-prints and asks her to massage his back. He likes to sand, to paint, to saw, install doors and cupboards.

August and September, the overalls Kari washes and hangs out on a clothesline that Johnny has put up.

With Howard, Johnny meets with men wearing suits in the bank, it's a part of the whole thing, they are offered coffee when they enter the bank premises, the girls who work there flirt in a discreet, almost pro-grammed way. Howard stands there boasting about the flats. There is one girl in particular whom he likes a lot. When the bosses step out of their offices to invite the cousins in, they ask the girls—in a flirtatious and slightly patronizing tone—to please not bother the cus-tomers with idle chit-chat. It is Howard who does the talking, for the most part; he is the one who has the full rundown, at least on the finances. Johnny becomes more and more blurry-headed from the whisky he is served, that he can't stand the taste of, but is expected to pour into himself as part of an unspoken ritual. Afterwards, Howard must drive the Impala and Johnny asks him to stop at the first and best place so he can buy a Coca Cola and get rid of the awful taste in his mouth. They swish through the streets wearing dark suits, with the bank's approval, with the bank's *blessing*, seated comfortably and securely in the enormous palm of the bank's hand, on the way to appointments with plumbers, carpenters and painters who call them sir.

When they top off the Sunday dinners with a little nightcap out in the backyard, they joke about how Howard never would have managed to wear work clothes and do carpentry work the way Johnny does. He can't even change a light bulb, Johnny says when Kari comes out to top up their drinks.

He says that it's not completely unthinkable that Howard was actually born wearing a suit.

On the occasions when Kari asks Johnny about the work at the textile factory, he assures her that it's not a problem. He asks her not to worry. He knows what he's doing. He has it all under control.

Rosenberg, Johnny says, he's got my back.

Ylva calls Kari and asks if they can meet. Kari hears a strange tone in her sister's voice, leaves the girls with her in-laws and takes the train to Manhattan. They meet at a cafe on Fifth Avenue and talk about each other's respective outfits for almost ten minutes before Ylva explains that Sigurd and Synnøve are talking about moving back to Oslo. They haven't made up their minds yet, but she thinks their father is tired of travelling so much. She says she doesn't know what to do. She doesn't know if she wants to move to Oslo and she doesn't know what she will do if she stays behind. Kari says that she is welcome to live with them, that she and Johnny have more than enough room. But her little sister replies with a polite, somewhat condescending, smile, as if what Kari has just proposed is not only inconceivable but also a little naive, a little foolish.

On the day of their departure, Johnny stands watching his in-laws embrace one another carefully, promising to write on a regular basis. His father-in-law shakes his hand and says please take good care of her, but the only thing Johnny can think about is how the exact same words are the title of an atrocious country song.

He stands there, as if on the outside of a circle.

Synnøve comes over and kisses him on the cheek, then turns back to Kari again immediately, and says something or other that Johnny of course doesn't understand. He sees Ylva clinging to her big sister, to America, to a life that she will return to in the future, return to again and again, every time insomnia poses its meaningless questions.

Kari is sad, in a way. It will be strange not having her mother and father and sister nearby. But then, she has Johnny. And the girls. And they can manage anything, right?

Of course they can, Johnny says.

Of course we can. And they can come and visit. Maybe we can even visit you, he says. I would like to see Norway.

He takes care of Kari. Gives her extra attention. Surprises her with small gifts and flowers and takes her along on drives as often as he can. When the new apartments are fully renovated, he asks her for advice and help, they have to be decorated, he says, and she is so good at that. Kari is more than a little proud when one night Johnny says that it's only fair that she, too, be paid for the work she does. They would have had to pay someone to do it anyway, he says. Men don't know a thing about stuff like that.

The bad luck begins when cousin Howard is found hanging in his apartment. In the long suicide note he admits to having embezzled money and writes in detail as well about a couple of incidents from his childhood that shock the family to such an extent that never again do they mention the summers they used to spend in upstate New York. Johnny doesn't know what to do. He goes to the bank. He thinks there is money but there is no money. He talks and drinks whisky and afterwards drives home slowly, while he tries to sort out all of the information the men in suits have served him in a pedantic tone of voice that makes him feel like an idiot. He thinks he understands most everything, that is what he tells Kari when she asks. He has it all under control, he says when Paul calls him and bothers him with questions that Johnny takes as attacks, as a dressing-down. He's not a child. He's not a little boy whom Paul can talk to however he wants. He gets into the car and drives out to Ocean Grove. He can't believe there is no money left. He tells the workers to keep working, before he finds himself inside an office at the bank, again, with a chunky glass of whisky in his hand. It's heavy, all of it, the glass weighs in his hand and Johnny nods and nods. He signs a number of papers, thinks he should ask about everything that isn't clear. He is tired. It will be fine, he says to himself, before slamming the car door shut and driving home.

There is a huge crowd of people standing outside an electronics store and staring at the television sets in the window display. He parks and gets out of the car. People are crying, hiding their faces in their hands. Someone has shot the president in the head. Johnny stands in the middle of the street. Around him everything is quiet. No cars making sounds. The sobbing cannot be heard. There is only a cold and paralysing silence.

In the New Year Johnny understands that it is impossible to make the payments. He has spoken with the insurance company. There is no money to be found anywhere. The bank is surprised by Johnny's supposed ignorance about his cousin's financial negligence. They look at him gravely, even suspiciously, and ask him a thousand questions that Johnny realizes he should have known the answers to.

When he thinks about Howard, he feels an enormous sadness, a true and raw grief, a tenderness that makes him struggle for breath as he remembers the image of his body dangling from the rafter in the kitchen. And then he thinks about the long summer holidays upstate, when he and Howard played with tin soldiers and fished in the stream and then Howard's suicide confessions cut through those memories like a razor blade.

He can't think about that. How could he have trusted a liar?

Billy talks him into going to Atlantic City. It's probably good to get away from all of it for a little while, he says. You need a little distraction. And that's what Kari says too, because Johnny has been nervous and distant for several weeks and she doesn't like seeing him like this. Kari and the girls wave them off on a Friday morning in April. When they come back to Asbury Park on Sunday evening, it is Billy who is driving the Impala, while Johnny sits in a rattling Dodge 1955 Royal that he has bought for god knows how much money. He drives it into the garage and the very next day he starts ordering parts and spending an unreasonable amount of time sitting with his head bowed over automobile magazines and manuals. Almost every day he drives off to buy overalls, new tools, oil, wires, rubber sleeves, hose clamps, cable boxes, silencers and spark plugs and ignition cables.

But there is no way out.

He loses the buildings to the bank, he feels ashamed, disenfranchized, chained to his own fear, to a feeling of impotency that he despises, as he sits and shakes like a snivelling child at the heart of his own fear.

Kari tries to stay positive for both of them.

It will be fine, she says. It's not the end of the world. There is always a way out, she says. And Johnny agrees. She is right. But he can feel the panic throbbing incessantly in his stomach. He decides to pull himself together, stand tall and look ahead. It can't be so bad, he thinks and repeats Kari's phrases to himself, word for word. But every time he comes back to dark thoughts. He thinks about the bank, about Howard, about the rafter, about the word *mortgage*. Then he scolds himself. Come on. Look ahead. Pull yourself together, dammit.

It's like flicking a switch.

From morning to night, in a spiral that he fails to find his way out of. Kari sits beside him, the girls are on his lap, the man he sees in the mirror has dry, grey eyes. One evening, after having sung some lullabies that Vera is particularly fond of, he sees a light, a hope, a true leg-up this time, an assurance that all this is temporary, that he and Kari and the girls can manage anything. That night he lies awake for a long time and talks, his voice is light, suddenly, he smiles in the darkness, he seeks out Kari's hand and holds her close. He'll just concentrate on work. The rest will sort itself out, eventually, he's sure about that.

It takes him an entire week to understand what has happened at the factory, a week during which he makes a fool of himself. When he tries to get started on the work that he has clearly neglected, it turns out that his father has replaced him, albeit not officially, but still, it makes him furious, makes him feel powerless and stupid. But even so, a whole week passes before he drives over to his childhood home. When Johnny finally goes, he tears off in a fury, preparing a monologue he thinks is sharp and powerful, but which he is still dreading to perform. He pulls up short in front of his parents' house and sees Paul come out onto the driveway, as if his father knew what was about to happen and wanted to secure the advantage.

I am the father, the father thinks. That is always an advantage.

But the son thinks the same thing, that the advantage is precisely in being the son. Johnny slams the car door shut and asks, yells, what *the hell* is going on over at the factory? He thinks the cussing is appropriate. He wheezes, he slaps the flat of his hand against the bonnet of his father's Chevy while demanding to know what the deal is with Rosenberg.

Stone-faced Rosenberg, who only repeated the same phrases over and over again: You will have to speak with Mr Richards, sir. I can't help you here. You'll have to speak with your father.

Paul looks right at Johnny, his eyes like two black marbles. Is he really so stupid that he didn't see this coming? What did he expect? That the whole world would sit by with their arms crossed waiting for him to finish playing his little game?

Oh, how that hurts.

Paul's body is like granite, a small, sturdy torso that stands in the way of everything. Doesn't his father see that Johnny has been trying to start something? Hasn't his father always taught him to believe in himself and what he is doing? Hasn't his father been reeling off such speeches ever since he was little?

Go for what you believe in, Johnny. Follow your dreams, Johnny.

Bullshit. All of it.

But his father refuses to let Johnny push this over onto his shoulders. He taught his son about responsibility, as well. And where has he been during the past year? Does he know anything at all about how the factory is doing? About who is and is not doing their job? If they are ahead or behind the production schedule? No, of course Johnny doesn't know, because he hasn't been there. He hasn't the slightest idea about the one thing he was supposed to have complete control over. And what now? What happens now, when his banker friends turn off the faucets?

Johnny calls him self-righteous. Johnny calls him prideful and smug and is so angry that he tells his father to shut up. He regrets it right away, but it's too late to turn back, so he keeps going, he knows that his father will hold this against him, that he's not going to forgive him for this lack of respect, but Johnny must continue, he has to believe that Paul will eventually understand that his rage is based on fear, that he is reaching out to him, hoping his father will help him out of this pinch. Is that too much to ask? *He* didn't mess up. It was Howard's fault. And in case Paul is worried about all of his fucking money, Johnny sure as hell won't be asking him for a thing, if that's what he thinks.

Not a single damn dollar.

Even when Dixie tries to intervene, they continue going at each other, father and son. An ancient battle is waged, by the garage, in the living room, under the lights of the expensive Italian lamps, while both pound their fists on the dining-room table, and compete to maintain the advantage both imagine they have.

Traitor. Irresponsible. Good-for-nothing. Immoral.

Your time has passed, deal with it. It's another world now.

Dreamer.

Your damn dreams.

You don't work for me any more.

Johnny finally ends up with a job at a tannery. Every single day he punches in at the four-storey, sooty, stone fortress on Central Avenue and 2nd Street. It is shit work. He softens, boils and dyes deerskin. He sorts and classifies hides, with time he also does depilation and degreasing. He stands for hours beside enormous water vats that spew out dirty water and every day he feels as if people are standing around and laughing behind his back.

That there's Johnny Richards.

Paul Richards' son.

What a damn loser. *He fucked up real good.*

Paul, he suffers as well, only in another way, because pain is like smoke, it can take on all shapes, get in everywhere. He suffers from the hardness he presents to his son, a hardness that has been passed on, which he himself inherited from *his* father. Oh, how he'd hated it when he was a child! How he'd despised it as an adolescent!

But now Paul sees it all differently.

It's for Johnny's own good.

It's important not to give in.

I'm suffering more than he is anyway, Paul tells himself when he wakes up at night from a dream, a long and outlandish dream where he is both his father and his son.

Dinner is still on the table when Johnny comes home. After eating, he takes a shower, stands under the gushing water with his eyes closed for a long time. He tries not to think. He concentrates on the sound of the water. He spends the evenings in the bedroom with the curtains drawn. He's tired, he says, and the girls have to be quieter and quieter.

The girls resemble Kari. And they resemble Johnny as well, they have the same stern gaze when they are hungry. She tries to speak Norwegian with them from time to time, but the girls answer in English.

They understand everything, Kari says, with a sort of resigned smile, to the neighbours. But they won't answer me in Norwegian.

In the bottom drawer of the nightstand, Kari has a hundred or so pieces of yellow paper. She writes to her father and asks for money, which she receives. Money that comes in handy and that Johnny doesn't want to know about.

They'll manage, she says.

They're young and they can manage anything, and even Johnny can see that, with a little help from her.

Look at our girls, Kari says.

Look at them and look at us. It's not so bad.

We can handle anything.

She writes long letters to her father. She likes to write letters, it's not just because of the money. The last thing she heard was that Ylva had fallen down a flight of stairs, that her mother had become completely addicted to all kinds of new electrical gadgets, and spent most of the day reading user manuals. As for him, he was always out travelling, her father wrote.

And of course, of course, he would send her a cheque. Everything will be fine. Johnny is a hard-working guy, isn't he?

At weekends Johnny is in the garage all day long. He eats his dinner in silence and the girls are quiet, too, when Daddy is like this.

That much they know.

Kari believes that love conquers all. She strokes Johnny's dark hair and says we'll manage. Your father is stubborn and so are you, she says. But we'll manage. If you don't want to apologize, she says, you must keep working the way you are now.

Johnny gets to his feet and says that he has nothing to apologize for, that he doesn't understand how Kari can be so *cold*.

Is it that simple? Do you believe everything is that simple? he asks, his voice choked with tears.

Yes, Kari says. We'll manage. This won't kill us.

But what am I supposed to do? Johnny says and is furious.

For him there is no greater silence than the answer to his own question.

The back streets in the evenings, full of boys and girls who bite and fight and kiss one another like beasts. In the summer the beach smells like candyfloss and seagulls and wet woodwork from boats named Kelly, Marilyn, Betty. They must tighten their belts. There's no way around it. Johnny sells the Dodge. They sell the house, after Kari's father has refused to give them another loan. Johnny is furious at everything and everyone. At his father. At himself. At Sigurd. But he disguises his rage as determination and Kari finds strength in this; she feels safe when he is like this, she says, although he can also be distant and unapproachable. They must search for a cheaper place to live and they find a house, finally, in Freehold.

We can live here, Kari says. She says she has a good feeling, that she can make it nice for them here, that she likes the garden.

The new house is smaller and the girls have to share a bedroom. Dixie comes to see them, bringing food and canned goods and money which she slips to her son with strict instructions not to say anything to Paul. But it's not enough. The girls grow out of their dresses. They need shoes. Johnny sells the Impala for a ridiculously small sum and afterwards he goes and gets drunk all by himself at a dive reeking of piss, before he goes to find Billy and snorts that a man without a car is not a real man. Billy listens to him and has a few beers as well, before he asks Johnny if he needs to borrow money and yeah, he does.

But all the same.

Johnny doesn't know what to do.

He falls and he falls.

Johnny is a man in free fall, far too frightened to open his eyes and look down at the ground rushing towards him.

Kari writes to her mother and asks for a loan. They don't want to sell the furniture, she writes. But it is Sigurd who writes back and the letter is full of exhortations about taking control of their own life, about responsibility and morality and about not giving up.

The next month she is desperate and calls Ylva. She has recently married a businessman from Halden. Her little sister tells her about the wedding and says that she missed them at the reception and Kari asks her to send photographs as soon as she can.

When it comes to the money, Ylva says she will talk to Gunnar as soon as he gets home from the auto show in Germany.

And the money Kari asks for comes.

But all the same.

They make friends with Terry and Mona who live across the street and who have a little boy who loves to play with the girls. When they get together Johnny becomes more light-hearted, he is able to relax, he and Terry have the same sense of humour and Kari insists that it's good for them to be around people, to spend what little time off Johnny has with others.

Terry says they can use his car and at weekends Johnny takes the girls to Asbury Park, to Keansburg or Spring Lake. They buy soda pop and pancakes.

Finally, Johnny walks the 18 blocks to Paul and Dixie's. His father is sitting on a stool in the garage. Johnny sits down. Says yes please to a beer. Fifteen minutes pass before he comes out again, humiliated, head bowed, but knowing that he won't have to work at the tannery for much longer.

It won't be like before, his father says and Johnny nods.

I know.

I can't make the same mistake twice. You'll be an ordinary worker. Is that understood? Do we have a deal?

Yes, he says.

He feels like a kid.

It won't be like before.

I know, Dad.

Neither Vera nor Ann notices the difference between the old and the new life. They play at their grandparents' house. At Terry and Mona's place. Out on the pavement and in the yard. They love being dressed up in identical dresses, as if they were twins. Vera holds Ann's hand when they cross the street and talks to her little sister the way Kari talks, in a mummy-voice. Dixie thinks that Vera is pretty enough to take part in a local beauty pageant for children, but Kari doesn't want anything to do with it and this is their first disagreement. Dixie is loud and sarcastic, and Kari, who has never seen her mother-in-law behave like this before, imitates her and fights back in kind. She talks even louder and ridicules her even more.

Johnny lets them carry on. He doesn't get involved.

Out in the garage he polishes his father's Chevy, which he is allowed to borrow. The rims and the bonnet and the doors. He polishes the floor mats with shoe polish, rubs them with old towels until they shine. His father doesn't say anything about the women's bickering either, nothing about what Johnny does or doesn't do with the car or with life in general. As long as he attends to his job. Paul hardly talks to his son any longer, but he talks to Kari about what's in the local newspaper. About street gangs and unemployment and about politicians who just lie and make promises they don't keep. Kari thinks that this is Paul's way of talking to his son. Through her. About things she couldn't care less about.

*

And the accident. The accident is just a step away, a small step in front of them, on the other side of these afternoons they spend in the new house, at home with Terry and Mona, at Johnny's parents' house.

That's the way of surprises.

They pop up out of boxes no one has been taught to notice. And afterwards, afterwards one remembers only the prelude, but for good measure, with a horrifying, cutting clarity.

They will remember that Johnny turned up the volume on the transistor radio, that Kari was giving both the girls a bath in the bathtub, where Vera made sure her little sister didn't get shampoo in her eyes. They will remember how the girls jumped up and down on their beds, while Kari dried their hair with clean towels that Johnny brought from the bedroom closet. They will remember the coffee-coloured nightgowns, the skinny arms that the girls raised up as high as they could while being dressed. They will remember Ann's sleepy eyes, little Ann who continued jumping even after she put on her nightgown, but who'd fall asleep the minute her head touched the pillow. They will remember that they told Vera to take good care of her little sister, to take her to the bathroom if necessary. Johnny stands in the doorway, watching Kari tuck in the girls, kissing them on their foreheads and then backing away towards him. Then they stand there for a moment and listen to Vera finish a long and breathless sentence. Good night, they say and then the girls wave. Then Johnny turns off the light and leaves the door open a crack. Kari is already on her way up the stairs, up to the bathroom on the second floor.

They will remember that Johnny gets ready in five minutes, while Kari has to put up her hair, try on different earrings, that she keeps coming in and out of the bedroom where Johnny is lying on the bed reading the newspaper. She asks about which shoes, which dress. He will remember her perfume, which she will never use again. They will see the short stroll over to Terry and Mona's house across the street. A slightly cold breeze. A plastic bag that never succeeds in taking flight, like a dog chasing its own tail on the pavement. They will remember Terry and Mona's living room and the welcome drinks. The evening will pass slowly, as if under water. Beer bottles on the table, the plans for a Sunday outing, the playful teasing about how Terry and

Mona must soon think about making another baby so that little Ronald can stop running after our girls.

Records and cigarettes.

The top hits of the day.

For a moment everything stands still, like in a drawing.

George Swensen is viewed with disdain by everyone at the party he has crashed, sick with jealousy, in a desperate attempt to speak to Judy Miller, with whom he had a brief but intense affair a year ago, and who is now with a man in a suit, an insignificant office rat from New York who doesn't even have money or friends with money.

This house looks like shit.

I wipe my ass with this party.

Come here, Judy, come here, come.

George Swensen tries taking a step towards where she is seated, on a sofa surrounded by men and cigarette smoke, by women wearing elegant dresses and holding tall glasses. As he takes a step in her direction, he is held back from behind by two men, he has no idea who they are.

Come out, you fucking Jew, George shouts when he turns around and throws a punch that momentarily knocks him off balance.

Someone asks him to calm down. Relax. Some even call him *sir* and their voices are friendly without being friendly, more scared shitless, damn sons of bitches.

From the corner of his eye he sees Judy standing up. He shoves someone, his elbow knocks against a cupboard or a radio. She is putting on her coat and George can see her green dress fluttering behind a doorframe. He looks at her stockings, at the black seam on the back of her calf and then he thinks about the mole that Judy has on her knee, which he once kissed like a crazy man.

Someone pushes him and he throws yet another punch into the air.

Judy leaves. She leaves with someone. George tears himself free from four pairs of arms and runs after her.

She leaves with someone else. He calls out to her, but Judy says she can't see him any more. He can't believe it. He follows after Judy and the man, runs out into the front hall and out the door. They are already out on the front lawn. George grabs a shovel that is lying in the flowerbed where a few white roses have been planted.

First he hits the office rat.

Once, spot on, in the back of the head.

The man drops to the ground and when he tries to stand up, the shovel hits him in the face.

George hears something crunch, like a sound he remembers from when he was a child, when he liked to lie down stretched out by a lamp post in the countryside and eat gravel.

Judy has turned around to face him. She stands there in horror, with one hand over her mouth, the other in front of her, as if she were trying to stop a car.

He hits her partly in the face and partly in the arm she is protecting herself with, before her friends take hold of him from behind and throw him to the ground. They pin him down, but he manages to kick one of them in the groin and thereby frees one of his arms. He strikes out and the punch hits an Adam's apple. When George manages to get to his feet, he gets hold of the shovel again and runs with it towards the car he has parked further down the street. The others are crouched down, taking care of Judy. One of them begins to move towards him, but George turns around and holds the shovel up like a baseball bat. Come on, motherfucker. Try me, he says, before getting into the car and disappearing.

He drives like a madman. Panting like a dog. On and off the highway. Passing petrol stations, red trees along the edge of the road. His hands, white knuckles, gripping the steering wheel. The New Jersey night above the low houses, in the blue and cool wind. He rolls down the window and calms down. Slows down and feels how his eyes slip. He thinks about Judy, slams on the brakes, rests his head on the steering wheel, feels sincerely sorry for himself for having lost her, for having sought her out even, for not having succeeded in winning her back. He steps on the gas pedal again.

Main Street. Murray Street. He turns the corner by the house where Kari and Johnny and the girls live. Ninety miles an hour, the tyres screeching against the pavement. (We heard it, all of it, Mona said afterwards, but we thought it was an ordinary accident).When George Swensen notices that he is losing control of the car, when the wheels hit the kerb, he closes his eyes, as if he is in the process of drowning and just gives in. He doesn't see that he drives straight through the picket fence painted green, over Vera's pushbike and a few toy shovels, over a tricycle and right into the wall of the house, of Vera and Ann's bedroom, where they are sleeping on their stomachs, with their arms dangling down over the sides of their respective beds.

The car is stopped by a tree behind the house, where Johnny has hung up a rope and a tyre, a kind of swing for the girls. It was as if the house was half eaten, Mona said later, to anyone who wanted to listen, because George Swensen's car had left a hole that looked like a mouth, a gaping mouth with hundreds of tiny teeth. Ann was found sandwiched between the tree trunk and the crumpled bonnet of George Swensen's Chevrolet. She lay sideways, as if she hadn't awakened but just continued dreaming whatever it is that children dream about. Vera was found by the left front tyre, her head had been squeezed in between the tyre and the fender, her body had been slung around and her head had been partially torn from her body. The reverend who had the thankless task of burying the girls, strongly advised Kari and Johnny against seeing them. He spoke about remembering life, not death; not the shadows, not the overwhelming silence, not the torn-up bodies. But Kari thought differently. She had to see the girls one last time, she said, almost without a voice, after some 60 hours without sleep, full of pills that mother-in-law Dixie had fed her. And in the belief that the type of grief she suddenly found herself in was *also* a painkiller, as if she carried a shield protecting her from all of it, as if she sat armoured behind a wall and nothing reached her, she managed to convince herself. It would do her good to see them. It was something she couldn't escape from. But when Kari walked down the stairs and into the cold room, when the young man pulled out the drawers and drew aside the white cloth over the bodies and Kari finally stood by her dead daughters, then she understood—unmistakeably— that life would never be good again. Never. This was the end, but she was condemned to go on beyond it. The end did not apply to her. The end would have been a relief, but this was anything but the end. She threw up. She ran and ran. She threw her body with all of her strength against a stone wall and, afterwards, sat and stared at god knows what for days.

Later, in the future that would come, she would not remember them one single time the way they were in the photographs, the way the girls were dressed up in

65

the summers when being happy was walking along the beach and the future lay open and the girls had not yet become this filthy mess that vaguely resembled children, small human beings, carcasses, entrails, half faces; a nose, a torn-up mouth, teeth, shattered eyeballs.

She comes home with her body full of cracks. She remembers nothing from the funeral. The fog moves, first across the cold earth, like a scratching, silent spirit between the graves of children, between black patent-leather shoes and the lawn and the crawling cars. And then up along her arms, shoulders, throat. She doesn't know who she is. Flowers appear, a dented iron vat of flowers in the centre of the table which is nauseatingly white. There are spots of rust on the ceiling. Her mouth is open. Someone takes hold of her arm and there are stains on the sky too, she sort of falls asleep and something races away with her body. The noise from the street, the noise from the pumping body, the words and all the hardness, like knife blades; the grief, a hole the size of a pinhead in the crevices of the heart. She lurches awake, as if she'd been pushed, and then she understands that she hasn't slept in several days. She walks down the stairs, sits in the living room and smokes cigarettes. The TV screen remains empty. A fly crawls across her hand. Hissing frogs moving up towards her mouth to suffocate her. It is her, still, with the green eyes. A dolphin hops through some iron rings. I want to sit here, just go to bed, she says to Johnny who is maybe standing there still, who may have left several hours ago, who is maybe a shadow, a tower, a reflection on the back of a spoon. Can she throw a glass to hell? Will it reach? The employees of the 24-hour chemist's stand smoking beneath a green neon cross. Pull down the blinds and erase the scene. Light a cigarette, protect the flame with the hollow of the hand, the wind that rushes across a beach. Who knows? The ocean grows little by little. The long hair has to go. Off with the long hair.

After the funeral, Ylva and Synnøve returned to Oslo but Sigurd stayed behind. He declined the offer to stay with Paul and Dixie and kept his room at the hotel. Every single morning for the next three weeks he had breakfast in his room before taking a taxi to Johnny's parents, where Kari and Johnny were staying temporarily. He was offered coffee, and after 15 minutes Kari came down the stairs, freshly showered, pale and thin, as if her clothes belonged to another person. He took her down to the waterfront. To the shopping centre, if it was too hot. They went to the cinema. In to Manhattan in the morning and back to Freehold late in the afternoon.

Her father said the only thing you could do was look to the future and Kari said that she didn't even understand what *to the future* meant any longer. In the evenings, Dixie would wait for them with dinner that she would heat up and then she would leave the room and let Kari and her father sit alone and eat.

I'll help you, sweetheart, her father said as they ate. I'll help you two. I know it doesn't help much to say so, but . . .

Daddy, please. I don't want to do this. Kari let her fork slide down onto her plate.

Sweetheart, I didn't mean . . .

Forgive me. Sorry. I'm just so tired.

Are you getting any sleep? Sigurd asked after a moment.

No, she said. But I'm tired. I need to sleep.

OK. I'll leave now, Kari. You try to get some sleep. I'll be back tomorrow.

I didn't mean it like that, she said. You can stay.

That's OK, he said. I have to make a few phone calls before I go to bed. He got to his feet.

It's been a good day, hasn't it?

Yes, Kari said. It has. Thank you.

Is there something you'd like to do tomorrow? Anything special?

No, she said. I don't know. What about you?

I thought that maybe we could go to . . . a museum, he said. It won't be long before I have to leave . . . it would be nice to . . .

Let's do that. That's fine, Kari said.

She followed him out into the hall, where he put on his overcoat and asked Kari to thank Dixie for dinner. When her father had left, she closed the door and stood there looking at some old shoes. Went into the living room. Her in-laws were sitting in the dark and watching television. Dixie smiled hesitantly. Johnny is out in the garage, she said.

I think I'll just go to bed, Kari said.

You do that darling, Dixie said, without taking her eyes off the television set.

Good night, Kari, Paul said. Try to get some sleep now.

Yes, she said. I will. Good night.

The night before Sigurd was to return to Norway, Dixie prepared dinner. After the main course, Sigurd asked if he might say a few words, stood up and thanked Paul and Dixie for all their support and love. It's at times like these that we need to have family around us, he said with tears in his eyes. Dixie tried to hold back her tears, but failed. Kari just stared in front of her, started shaking and hyperventilating, and Johnny had to take her to her room and give her even more of the pills that Dixie claimed helped.

Then they sat there, like ghosts, without saying anything for a long time. When Dixie got up to clear the table and do the dishes, Paul recalled that he had in fact got hold of a bottle of Norwegian aquavit for the occasion.

They retired to the living room. It was a relief to be pulled out of the silence.

Paul filled the glasses, Sigurd and Johnny raised them ever so slightly, as if even the act of toasting together was disrespectful, as if by simply living they were mocking the girls. Paul filled the glasses. They drank, they emptied the glasses and drank again. The grief ran through them like electricity, like something caught in a closed circuit.

Finally Dixie sat down with them. Said yes please to a glass of aquavit. Sigurd talked about the difference between potato spirits and wheat spirits, about caraway seeds, anise, dill and fennel. The others nodded, relieved about not having to speak. They were tired, everyone had dark circles around their eyes, slag around the heart.

Sigurd talked so he wouldn't really have to talk. They others pretended to be interested. Upstairs, on the second floor, Kari lay in bed. If Sigurd even thought about his daughter it was like something inside him slid out of joint.

So he continued.

He told them about taffel aquavit and brown aquavit and equator aquavit.

Paul refilled the glasses. Sigurd told them about the food traditions of Western Norway. About raspeballs, about roast hare and red-currant wines. When he mentioned sheep's head, Dixie said, oh yes, I remember you told us about the sheep's head. Oh, Sigoord, it sounds just awful, I'm sorry.

Dixie decided it was time for her to turn in. They couldn't sit here talking about decapitated heads. They just couldn't.

Paul refilled the glasses.

Johnny went to the toilet and when he came back, the two men sat looking at him as if he had returned from a long journey.

What is it? he said to his father.

What do you mean? Paul said.

Don't pull that with me, Johnny said. I know you. What is it?

Well now, said Sigurd and took over. Paul and I have been talking a little over the past few weeks . . .

Is that right?

That's right, we have been talking and . . . You know this is difficult for all of us, Johnny. This . . . it's unreal and . . . it's difficult . . . I don't mean . . . not that there's any solution . . . but what *can* we do, you know? That's what one asks oneself, every day. What can we do?

One has to give it time, Paul said.

That's right, Sigurd said. That's right. There is no way around it.

What are you talking about? Johnny said again, addressing his father.

Well now, Paul said, but he was interrupted.

We thought that perhaps it might be good for you to live in Norway for a time, Sigurd said. I know that it's not going to solve anything at all. Believe me, Johnny. But maybe it would be good for Kari, yes, for both of you, to get away from . . . yes, from this.

We're worried, all of us, Paul said. She has lost so much weight and she doesn't sleep and . . .

I know, Johnny said. There was a frailty in his voice, a tenderness that he himself could hear and that made him infinitely sad. I know, he repeated.

I'm worried about my daughter, Sigurd said. I fear for her, Johnny.

Me, too, Johnny said, and was unable to hold back the tears. Sorry, he said.

Don't worry, his father-in-law said. Let it out. Just let it out.

Paul filled the glasses.

We'll help out as best we can, his father-in-law said. Think about it, Johnny. Maybe it's a good idea. Another life. Maybe it will help in the long run.

What do *you* think? Johnny asked and looked at his father.

It's your decision, up to both of you. But I think Sigurd is right. And I won't let you down this time, son, Paul said, his voice breaking. I promise.

Thank you, Johnny said and reached over to his father and hugged him as hard as he could. Thanks.

The nights were the worst. Kari turned off the light, rolled over and lay there, waiting. For the night to yield. For the silence to be broken. Her face to the wall. Waiting for daybreak so she could get up and be spared lying in this darkness, in this swamp of a bed, impaled by her daughters' deaths. The echo of the girls in every single pore of her skin, in every single corner of her in-laws' house. The house as if covered with veils of grief. Something spider's web-like. The stale, heavy air. The curtains drawn, the radio turned off, whimpers; Paul breaking down in the bathroom when he caught sight of his grandchildren's bath toys; Kari who suddenly started howling in the living room, in the kitchen, in the backyard; Dixie who was unable to stop sobbing and who in vain lay biting her pillow at night so no one could hear her.

Daytime. Every bit as intolerable as the night. As everything else. Every single second that she lay awake was an agony she did not understand how to endure. She got up after having lain sleepless for weeks, in the same bed as Johnny, but all the same far away, in her own end of the grief. She dressed herself slowly, the madness pursuing her like a hornet. Everything, every single tiny thing, required the utmost exertion. I can hardly breathe, she thought one night, when everything seemed unending and shapeless and sticky. She walked back and forth in the house with heavy steps. Into the bathroom. Water on her face. Out into the garden. In again. On with her shoes and out into the garage. Eating as if asleep, awake on the third day. The feeling of her eyelids stinging. Throwing up her food, pushing around a shopping cart that is heavy and awkward, and she suddenly starts to scream, to wail in the supermarket, and a security guard comes over to Johnny who tries to calm her down in the aisle between the shelves of food.

You will have to take her outside, sir, the guard says and Johnny drags his wife out while the other customers stand and watch them as if from the other side of a photograph.

At what point does a human being lose his grip and the brain go blank? What's it called, everything that is hanging from the walls, covering up the lamp and the light from the lamp, covering the walls with greenery, and the stomach and the heart and the lungs with rot?

Johnny borrows his father's car and drives around aimlessly.

Shark River Park. Neptune. To Farmingdale and back again. Hudson Street, Spring Street, Murray. He parks the car on McLean Street and crosses the car park. The sun blinds him. Everything is white in this light, almost erased. I'm fading away too, he thinks, has to stop and lean against a tree. He walks down along Country Road like a zombie. Some kids cycle past him outside the fire station. He crosses the street without looking and is almost hit. The driver yells at him, but Johnny barely reacts. He turns around and walks into a church that is almost empty. There he sits like a fool and stares up at a crucifix. For the first time since his childhood, he talks to God. Why? he asks. Why us, exactly? he asks. What's the point?

Who are you, really?

He goes to church with his mother. He doesn't know whether it helps. He doesn't know anything. He is greeted with hugs and pats on the shoulder. It's terrible, says the baker from the corner. He meets Mona and Terry, whom he hasn't seen since the funeral and who sit with him and Dixie, but barely manage to look at him. He doesn't blame them. He knows there is something in him that is monstrous. The next Sunday he brings Kari with him. She wears a dark dress that makes her beautiful in a ghost-like manner. At church she accepts condolences from neighbours and acquaintances. She reaches out her hand. Her eyes are almost completely white. Her face, like a plaster mask. They meet Terry and Mona and their little boy. They sit in the same pew. Johnny folds his hands and closes his eyes. Every time he feels the tears welling up, he looks up at the sailboat that is hanging down from the ceiling of the church. As if the tears will then recede, back into the hollow space behind his eyes. He envisions caves, dead water, paper boats. He tries to breathe calmly. When the reverend gives his sermon, he finds Kari's hand and holds it tightly, as if to say something that he can't identify for himself. He looks up at the boat, imagines the ocean and waves breaking against the pier Vera liked to throw stones from. He tries not to think about waves, the sky, about the green spot in Ann's left eye. He sees the reverend without seeing the reverend. He half listens. Everything goes round and round.

It is 1967. The summer of love.

It's no use.

He makes tea and slices up Dixie's cranberry pie, convinces Kari to sit out in the backyard with him. It's starting to get cooler now, finally. He has brought along a quilt and a candle and sits within the sound of insects, of the odd car driving past the house. Kari says that she feels as if she is about to crumble up here, but Johnny says we can manage anything. Now it's his turn to say it and he repeats the phrase until it sounds hollow and strange. Afterwards he embraces her. He holds her long and hard, but Kari does not stop trembling. He puts the quilt over her shoulders.

We can manage anything, you and I.

But it's not true and he knows it.

He, too, wants to collapse, like a marionette.

Kari looks up at the sky. It is black and sparkling. I can't do this, she says while the tears fall. Her face is completely calm. No twitches around her mouth. The tears just keep coming. She has ceased thinking about her own tears.

We can manage anything, he says. But the nights suffocate him too. And New Jersey suffocates him and he says maybe they can do something else. They will have to do something. Something else. Not because they are going to run away from anything, but because maybe it will do them good.

Do you think? Kari says.

Yes, Johnny says, I think so, and he clutches her hand and can feel her making an effort and squeezing his, a tiny pressure, only, fingers that twist into one another as if to say thank you or yes, or help me, and one day, several months later, one day they decide, look into each other's eyes and say yes, yes, yes and then Kari and Johnny land at Fornebu Airport, their broken-down life in tow. They get off the plane, their breath steaming frost, and they fix their gazes upon the clouds over the Oslo Fjord.

PART TWO

I can't help it. That's how we talk to each other. It's how we've always talked to each other, even before, even when I almost couldn't talk because I was so young. I always paid attention. I was an observant child. Did I mention that? I was the kind of child who had to pay attention, who found out too many things. Mum and Dad came to Norway. That's how that part of the story goes. That's how Dad began and that's how Mum began. They decided they wanted to have a new life.

Grandmother and Grandfather and Aunt Ylva and Uncle Gunnar stood in a semicircle waiting for them at Fornebu Airport on the afternoon they arrived. I can imagine them hugging one another for a long time. That Mum cried. Uncle Gunnar took a picture that I've seen—Dad with a suitcase in each hand going out the glass doors, towards the car park. Then they drove in towards Oslo on a little road that Dad later learnt was the motorway, what they called a motorway in Norway. Buildings and construction sites, a marina, the white dinghies like children's shoes, the black water and the fog that would not lift.

That's how Dad told it, but he didn't say what kind of fog it was.

I never knew whether what he was speaking about was real fog.

I asked. I always asked about hundreds of things. I said: Daddy? And he said, yes kid, what is it?

And then I made up a question. I asked if it was real fog and he replied that he looked out the car window, that the others switched over to speaking Norwegian, that the Norwegian language was like sounds from an alien machine. He looked at Mum. She sat between Aunt Ylva and Grandmother, and he thought it was nice listening to her, nice to see her sitting there and pronouncing sounds that he didn't understand at all.

They were her sounds, kid. Her family's sounds.

That's how he answered.

And I nodded and then he went on talking and I forgot the fog, I forgot about it until the next time he told me the same story. Then I remembered it again and asked: Daddy, was it real fog? And he replied that afterwards they had eaten waffles and drank coffee in the flat that Grandfather had put down a deposit on. What an awful word, he said. He had asked how they were going to manage to pay their way. It was the first evening in Norway and Grandfather had said that they would figure it out, that they could talk about it later.

That's how Dad answered. A coffee table. A coffee cup and waffles shaped like hearts. He had got up and gone to the toilet. He had taken off his shoes and it made him feel foolish, like a child. He didn't like walking around in his stocking feet. Never. Not later on either. After I was born. He didn't like taking off his shoes in other people's homes and at home he always kept his shoes on. They fought about it, later, he and Mum. Then I was older and knew everything about my sisters and it was around that time when Mum wasn't well, before she became happy and contented and before Dad left.

*

All of it, as if viewed through a bottle. The room where he and Mum would sleep, the room that from then on was their bedroom, the lamps and the nightstands, the burgundy carpet and the sofa and chair set in the living room. So different. The candlesticks and the folded napkins. Aunt Ylva who had grown up, become a woman, that was what Dad said. A woman who looked at him with compassionate eyes, but she couldn't be blamed for that. Grandmother who went in and out of the kitchen, poured coffee, brought cookies, carried out a tray of cups and saucers and asked about the flight, about the food on the plane and about what Dad thought of the in-flight service. There are photographs. Dad is wearing a yellow jumper. He is so pale, his lips are so red it almost looks as if he's wearing lipstick. Grandfather by the door to the balcony, pointing at the construction site below the block of flats, patting Dad lightly on the shoulder.

It was always late in the evening and I asked. But Dad said that I had to sleep and I said that I wasn't tired, even though my eyes stung and I kept yawning. He said that he'd seen a church on the way up to the neighbourhood of Bekkelaget, a church that he later never found again.

What else? I asked.

The fortress, he said. Akershus Fortress. It was magnificent.

They sat and drank coffee. He excused himself, wanted to go for a walk in the new neighbourhood. Grandfather offered to go with him, but Dad said he would prefer to go by himself. Clear his head. It had been a long trip.

And outside it was so cold. It smelt like aluminium. A few weeks later the snow began to fall. The Ekebergsletta field looked like a sleeping white whale. Dad woke up while it was still dark, to the sound of snowploughs. Afterwards the silence was enormous. He got up and went down to the store. He saw children who looked like cartoon astronauts in their enormous snowsuits. Children who played. Children who dug themselves in and out of expanding snowdrifts at the kindergarten. Bekkelaget was full of children and the cold cut into him. He shivered and shivered and when he came back to the flat, he turned up the electric-panel heaters until Mum started turning them down again, saying no, we can't afford it.

And then what happened? I said.

Well, he said, the afternoon came and the evening and the weather changed, summer came and so on. Go to sleep now, sweetheart. That's enough for now.

In the beginning they got up early every day, he and Mum. Everything was going to start over. The new life, Dad had said, and Mum had repeated it.

The new life.

But only a few weeks had passed and Mum sat down in the kitchen to smoke and look out the window and then she started sleeping late in the morning because there was nothing she was supposed to do anyway. Dad went into the bedroom to wake her up and tell her that it was already noon or one or even two o'clock. Sometimes, when the sun between the neighbouring buildings came out, the kitchen was lit up and

Mum's hair shone even more than usual and he thought that maybe she was the one giving off all of this light.

They had decided to lie to each other, Mum said many years later, after the guy from Bergen had mostly stopped coming around and everything kept going to hell more and more often. She took me in her arms in the evenings, when I came home. There she sat, as freshly made up as when I'd left her. Then she wanted to talk. She still does that sometimes. Her mouth always smells and she wants me to sit and talk a bit with her before I go to bed. Then she talks about Dad. And her eyes become as yellow as an Indian's and then she looks at everything else but me when she tells me things I already know: about the flat in Bekkelaget, about the winters back in the day, and about Dad's gaze, restless and erratic. Dad made coffee and they talked. His face was wax-like. He was so fragile, your father. He told her about his dreams—he dreamt about ash and sand and a full moon that clawed its way up the Oslo Fjord. He dreamt about children who walked in circles in the cemetery down in Nordstrand, and he dreamt that somebody had tied a rag around his face, a gauze bandage that kept his mouth and lips closed.

Just foolishness, you know, all of it.

They slumped together in their own living room, in hushed and gentle tears, in kisses that were cautious, in embraces so fierce that they came to be afraid of each other. All of this I know. Breathing against the other's breath. A chest that began to shudder. Kissing over tears, how they consoled each other and refused to let go. Mum walked around in her slippers. She washed clothes, hung up clothes, folded clothes. She was getting things ready, she said. Had to get things ready. She went into the bedroom, made the bed, organized all of the clothes in the closets, looked at everything Dad had brought with him from America, everything that he hardly ever wore any more—T-shirts, sweatshirts and jeans that were either too small or out of style.

And then what happened?

The salty taste of your mother, Dad said. She woke up all of a sudden, and was drenched in sweat and sobbing. She sounded like a tortured animal. Dad had turned on the light and got really scared when Mum was unable to stop. But afterwards she came back to him. Afterwards they lay in bed with the light on, because she didn't want him to turn it off again.

It all starts here, in my stomach, she had said.

It didn't do her any good staying home. Dad just wanted her to get up. He wanted the new life to begin. He wanted Mum to let her hair grow out and get up, out of bed. But the past was a nightmare she'd stepped out of, like a contorted witch, one of these innocent, young girls sheared in shame, to be burnt on the bonfire of history.

That was how he answered.

Finally Grandfather found her a part-time job as a receptionist at a law office in the city centre. And so Mum went to work and came home from work, and Dad started helping Grandfather with odd jobs. Nothing out of the ordinary, he said. He was asked to put address stickers on envelopes, type address lists or find telephone numbers in the phone book. Sometimes he had to go out to Bygdøy and help out in the garden or in the woodshed, but he told me that he never really grasped what it was he did to earn the money he had started receiving every month. The times when he asked Grandfather directly, the answers were always evasive. Mum said he should just be thankful for the money, that they needed it, that something or other would turn up sooner or later.

Poor Dad.

He sounded so stupid when he spoke Norwegian. He smiled like a fool when he didn't understand what people said. When he laughed because he thought he was supposed to. He told me that he had tried to learn some words and phrases in the beginning. And he could talk to people, it wasn't that. But he smiled like a fool when he understood too. This language doesn't fit in my mouth, he said to me later.

When spring came, the first spring here, then Grandfather took him on hikes in the woods of Nordmarka, lent him shoes and trousers and a backpack which Dad filled up with whatever he was told. He thought that he looked like a clown. He tramped over branches and stones. The woods never opened, the smell of it was dense and rancid, the stupid shoes sinking deep into the damp moss. Grandfather tried to teach him the names of trees and birds in Norwegian and Dad repeated the words: *Hegre, måke, gjøk, ugle, tiur, lønn, furu. Skjennungstua, Kikut, Svarttjernshøgda, Sandungen, Gjerdingen, Katnosa.* They walked and walked and he couldn't understand where they were going. But finally they arrived. There was nothing there. Just more of the same. Trees and stones and the wind that only just drowned out the black birds. He made an effort. They ate their packed lunches in silence, while sitting on stones or wooden benches.

The pregnancy came as a surprise. I learnt that from Mum, the times she talked in exactly the same way as when she threw up the liquor and the soups I had made for her, when a few days had passed since she had eaten and I had to use my young hands to force open her mouth. All of this I learnt in between heaves—after my sisters were killed, they almost never slept together, because every time it happened, Mum said, every time their bodies approached in the dark, enormous distances arose; it was miles from her hands to his, between her hips and his thighs. When she threw back her head and closed her eyes, it was as if she closed an iron gate. He lay on top of her, she reached out a hand and took hold of his neck, but it was like grasping at empty air. Even when she got up and they changed places, even when Mum sat on top of Dad and opened her eyes and released all of her weight upon his chest, even then they were like two statues, two blocks hitting against each other.

But there was no sound.

This is what I had to listen to, here in Bergen, in between heaves, with Mum in my arms, with Mum bent over the sink, in the mirror in the bathroom, with Mum all the way into the cold room where she saw my sisters and everything that came afterwards; vomit, vomit, vomit.

Dad put down his newspaper, sat with her, stroked her hair and lay his head on her swelling stomach. He did his best to distract her. He knew what she was thinking, because he was thinking the same thing.

Would I manage to live? Would I manage to cope and survive?

Mum wanted to get some air and Dad got dressed and went with her, even though he was cold. They went for short walks. Up and down to the school. Over to

Ekebergsletta field and back. The new life had to be lived and Dad wanted to glimpse some kind of joy in her, when he caressed her stomach with his hand, when he brought her along to the city to buy a pram and baby clothes, when he used what strength he had to overlook the ghosts that cast shadows over the main street Karl Johans gate, the Stortorvet Square, ghosts that glided across the vacuum of the sky like mutilated angels. My sisters must have been everywhere, deformed children with wings full of wounds, yellow, aching wounds, the stench of which reached Mum and Dad like the thud of a steady knocking, as if branded upon their life.

It's not easy, Dad said one day, when Mum asked why he didn't speak Norwegian with people.

But nothing was easy, even if it looked that way. It wasn't easy to accept money. Not easy to feel how the autumn rain clung to the body, not easy to see winter approaching. It wasn't even easy for them to look each other in the eyes any more.

One day Mum found him standing in the living room with his eyes shut.

He took hold of her hand.

He said that he loved her more than anything else, but Mum only heard fear, like a silver rim around his words. And she twisted free, carefully, but smiling, as if she were playing.

And then what happened?

Yes, what happened then?

Her stomach grew and the weather changed, summer came and so on. Now you must sleep, Marita.

Please.

Her stomach grew. They tried to find the simplest way of living. The spoke to each other kindly. In daily life. They did not ask each other a single time during the course of her pregnancy whether I might be a girl or a boy. They pretended nothing was wrong. The flat was where they could silence the life out of anything. Dad sat in the office, Mum in the kitchen or in the living room. At night they went over all of it again, by themselves, moment by moment, drink by drink over there at Terry and Mona's.

The sound of the rubber tyres and everything afterwards.

In the middle of the night, Mum dreamt of lorries, about uniforms preserved in formaldehyde, she dreamt that somebody washed off a pavement after an accident. She told me about these dreams later. The moon was on the telly all the time. Mum dreamt of the remains of a house, scraps of carpet, bedposts, closet doors and shoes. She dreamt about scarves and umbrellas and the 1960s like a load she had to drag around with her for ever, like a cart that would just grow heavier and heavier. Once she dreamt about a ship where she was the captain. She dreamt that she had two boys.

Two young boys who were alive, boys with shiny, adorable faces.

I was born in the middle of the summer of 1969, at Ullevål Hospital, following labour that lasted for almost 20 hours. Mum came home with her body full of stretch marks, it burnt, her hands lifted me up and nothing felt worse than breastfeeding me, nothing worse than the nausea that surged up when I took hold of the nipple and grew quiet and she had to look everywhere except at me, anywhere except at my mouth and my wide-open eyes and hands that waved back and forth and clutched at the air, that opened and closed around something invisible.

My first memory is of a glass of water on Dad's nightstand. It was on top of a book and I knocked it over. It didn't break, but the water ran down onto the carpet and I ran out and told Mum right away. It is the first glimpse I have of the world. The room was completely blue, or so I imagined later, even though I knew that their bedroom wasn't.

Dad went with me on the first day of school. And he was so clumsy, poor thing. He did everything so quickly. He forgot to tuck my jumper down into my stockings properly, so I sat and froze all day even though it was the end of the summer. That's why I look so cross in the picture. I told him on the way, but maybe he was nervous or maybe I just thought that I had told him or we were running late. He went with me into the classroom, and afterwards went on his way. I sat and watched him through the window to see if he had hidden himself some place. I can't remember what Mum was doing. Why she wasn't there.

Sometimes we took the tram down to the city and went out to visit Grandmother and Grandfather in Bygdøy. Grandfather always sat me on his lap and ever since I was very young he would slip me coins. Spend them well, he said. I liked that. And I liked the big house and the garden and how quiet and dark it was in there. Aunt Ylva had just had Julie; she and Uncle Gunnar had struggled for a long time to make a baby, that was why they'd filled the house up with dogs. That's how I remember it anyway. That Julie had just been born and that the grown-ups used to sit and talk for hours around the dinner table while they passed her back and forth among themselves. I was left to wander around the house alone. And the further away from the living room I got, the quieter it was. I especially liked playing under the stairway that went up to the first floor. I used to sit there with my dolls or with the gifts I always received when I came to visit. Once, Aunt Ylva had been abroad and bought some red patent-leather shoes for me, which I thought were the nicest I had ever seen. A few months later they were too small, but I still insisted on wearing them and one day I came home from school with my feet full of open blisters. Two of my toes were almost completely black.

Sometimes, we went to Aunt Ylva and Uncle Gunnar's house too, especially at weekends. But I was afraid of their dogs, even though they were always in a cage when we arrived. Once, Aunt Ylva served a soup with egg in it and I thought it tasted terrible and asked if it was dog food. Mum yelled at me, even after Aunt Ylva had said that it didn't matter. And a few days later, when Dad and I were down on Karl Johan in the city centre, standing there with our hands over our ears as the local marching band came parading by, Dad said that he thought it had tasted awful as well and that he thought it tasted like dog food too, but we mustn't tell anyone.

Grandfather used to take me along on hikes in the woods. Me and Mum. They put gloves on me and a hat and we walked up to Ullevålseter Lodge, and I didn't like it. Daddy never came along. Grandmother sometimes did, but often it was just Grandfather and me and Mum. I didn't like it at all. For my sixth birthday I got a pink bicycle that I rode all the time, the whole summer and the whole autumn. When it started snowing, I wanted to just keep cycling around but Mum said no. One day when she was at work, Dad gave me permission to ride my bike indoors. First, I helped Dad move the coffee table and the dining-room table and then we cleared things out of the hallway and then I could ride back and forth between the bathroom and the kitchen.

Afterwards, we put everything back in place again and were snickering behind Mum's back all evening, until she exploded and I was sent to my room. I could hear them arguing through the walls. Dad came in after a while, tucked me in and read to me. I fell asleep, but a little later the sound of one of them crying woke me up—I couldn't tell who it was—and I was scared to death. It was the first time that I'd heard a grown-up cry. I'd never imagined that they could cry.

One day Dad said to me: If you don't feel like going along to the woods, you can just stay home with me. You don't have to go.

But I had to go along once in a while. Other times I wouldn't budge and was allowed to stay home.

It was as if I was being tugged at and I didn't like that.

Once in a while Paul sent American newspapers and magazines in the mail. Dixie always put a little bit of money in the envelope, tucked away in one of the magazines. *Time. Newsweek. Life.* Johnny read slowly to make the contents last as long as possible. He sat on the toilet and read month-old editions of the *New York Times*. It made no difference. Sometimes Billy sent *Playboy* magazines, which Johnny hid in the storeroom in the cellar, and took out when he was home alone during the day. Billy would also include a letter or a note; he told of how things were going with The Doc and with Luke and with Tina. He wrote that they missed him, that he would have to come and visit soon. Johnny leafed through the pages. Charles Manson, the satanic slayings, knife blades and foetuses. The Dallas Cowboys met the Miami Dolphins in the Super Bowl. Nixon. Vietnam. Street people arrested for eating dogs in East Harlem. Altamont and Janis Joplin and Johnny who reaches for Kari with hands of ash. The nostalgia is not dried flowers scattered across the bed but his father's old Chevy, the mornings on the couch while the rain replaces the sun which replaces the rain. The nostalgia is not dried flowers but an alarm clock, the reflection of a car mirror, a Coca Cola sign, ordinary things. Paul in the garage or Dixie in the kitchen wearing an apron and with curlers in her hair. A light pressure against the chest, as if a hand were on its way up to the throat. It's a kind of amalgam, the nostalgia. Sometimes it's hard to know. Sometimes things run together and Johnny finds himself walking around the snow-covered Oslo streets, in the spring light in the old town of Gamlebyen, on the tram, as tired and sentimental as a washrag; he imagines Dixie and the house, dry leaves hanging from the trees where he carved out the names of girls with knives and nails. He sees the intersection on Lincoln Avenue, Billy who is almost run over one morning when the clouds are almost completely black, like beetles against the deep blue sky. The sun pops up at the end of the Oslo Fjord, in the uppermost corner of the tram window. Johnny reaches out his hand towards the light, towards an estate agent in upstate New York, towards a billboard advertising make-up on the highway to Freehold.

He tugs the tram cord.

The new life.

The new life has been going on for years.

At home, Marita goes around simultaneously pulling things to pieces and mending them. At home, the little girl opens her eyes wide and learns all the words Johnny has to teach her. She runs between the kitchen and the living room. Between Mother and Father, between Daddy and Mummy, between Ann and Vera.

The new life.

Johnny has seen Stryn and the Geiranger Fjord and the Jostedal Glacier. He has taken the Røros railway and the Bergen railway and travelled across Stord, through Bømlo, onward to Haugesund and Stavanger. He likes the mountains and the fjords and the narrow roads. He likes the deep forests, the openness of Eastern Norway. It reminds him of America.

But the winter darkness is tenacious, the slushy pavements, this feeling of walking around and stepping on things that decompose. The Norwegian reality, daily life feels so remote, even though he is living in the midst of it. He reads the newspapers. He watches television, tries to stay informed about what's happening. But still. Something fundamental is missing, a kind of connection between him and the country.

Luckily I have the two of you, he says, and sometimes Kari is still able to kiss him, to stroke his hair and then a kind of fog lifts.

When Marita was two years old, a young couple moved in on the fourth floor and Johnny and Kari were invited to the house-warming party. The late summer evening was cloudless and full of light. The door to the balcony was wide open and the curtains moved in the sunlight, on gentle gusts of wind. After a few hours people started to change. Petter Johnsen, the handball coach, got so drunk that he did a nose dive right into the coffee table. But instead of asking him to calm down—instead of walking him out and asking him to go home and get some sleep or coffee—Johnsen became the life of the party, with his shiny eyes and rough, pirate-like laughter. He howled, sounded like a braying drunk from another century. Tove Furuset, who was so shy that she virtually trembled when she met people on the stairway, suddenly become loud and talkative and lost her balance at one point, knocking down a lamp as she fell. The same thing happened again—people laughed. Johnny went to the toilet and saw two neighbours standing and groping each other in a bedroom where the door was open a crack. In the living room the music was turned up until it was no longer possible to talk and Johnny ended up sitting in a corner of the couch with Gerd Fjeld—a matron-like cashier who for the occasion had put on a completely horrendous dress—who rested her huge masculine hand on his thigh and spit into his ear when she talked; they were *so* happy to have an American in the building, she said (she didn't say why); he was *such* a handsome man, she said and then she screamed and howled out phrases in Norwegian to the other guests, before once again turning back to Johnny and repeating what she had already said in different ways.

He had tried to make contact with Kari, but she was sitting too far away. She lit a cigarette and blew the blue smoke up towards the ceiling lamp, towards the open balcony door, where darkness had now fallen. And the moon, the moon on a string, surrounded by everything Kari blew in its direction.

And then she had danced.

He had tried to make contact with her, but her gaze had slipped away. He had even tried signalling her with his hand, but then she'd turned around and laughed with the man beside her, and her smile afterwards was odd, cardboard-like, as if painted on. And then Johnny had wanted to go over to her, but she moved out to the middle of the living room, closed her eyes and started waving her arms. The music and Kari and the stupid movements. Johnny just stood there. He could barely stand to watch. It looked as if she was about to fall backwards, down into a hole, slowly, as if the speed had been turned down. Her arms. Her hips and waist and eyes closed beneath the eye-shadow. Eventually Johnsen had got to his feet and Kari had let him stand there writhing up against her.

He finally managed to bring her home. They ended up standing and arguing in the hallway, while they took off their shoes. She was sullen. Drunk and irritated, and called him a fucking wet blanket. It was the first time he had heard the phrase in Norwegian. Kari stormed into the kitchen. Opened a bottle of wine. The eye-shadow. The silence when Marita stayed with her grandparents. The empty flat, just the two of them. The eye-shadow when she poured herself a drink. She had danced. She had stood on the far edge of something, with her eyes closed. With Johnsen. With Johnsen behind her like a wall. The blue eye-shadow and her hips. She danced and everything went down wrong, got stuck in his throat.

His father-in-law found him a temp position as an English teacher at Uranienborg School. Starting in the autumn he would work at the school four days a week. Johnny said that he was happy about it and, in a way, he was. He needed to get out of the house. But he was not sure whether he would do a good job, he said. He had never taught anything whatsoever.

It's just kids, his father-in-law said. It will be fine.

And it was.

Johnny had two eighth-grade classes. He liked the pupils for the most part. And they thought it was exciting that the teacher was from the US and not just some Norwegian or other with lousy pronunciation. The teacher who was on long-term sick leave, whom Johnny was replacing, gave him a curriculum of sorts. The other teachers gave him suggestions, he leafed through the English books, let the pupils read out loud and corrected their pronunciation. He sat in the teachers' lounge, smoked cigarettes and listened to stories that he did not always understand. There were always a large number of gaps in the stories, black puddles where things disappeared. He could understand the people from Oslo. It was worse with some of the others, a slightly older teacher from Stavanger, for example, who often sat with him while she ate her packed lunch. Worst of all was the math teacher from Lom, whom Johnny did not understand at all, who had been to the US a number of times and who also loved to talk about everything he had experienced there.

At least that's what Johnny thought.

He still felt like a slow pupil. That's how it always was, on the occasions when the other teachers addressed him and took care not only to speak slowly, so Johnny could understand, but also more loudly, as if he had difficulties with both the language and with his hearing. And when that happened, all of the other conversations fell silent and everybody looked at him with a mixture of pity and mild irritation.

The summer of 1972 Paul and Dixie came to visit. They spent three weeks in Norway and stayed with Sigurd and Synnøve, who were only too happy to have them. There was no point in spending a lot of money on a hotel when the house was as big as it was.

Marita had made two flags—one Norwegian and one American—which she waved when Grandpa Paul and Grandma Dixie appeared in the arrival hall at Fornebu Airport. She wanted to sit on Dixie's lap on the way in from the airport but that wasn't allowed. She could, on the other hand, sit between her grandparents in the back seat, Johnny said. Paul found it foolish that it wasn't the owner of the car who decided where people could and could not sit. Dixie had brought with her an entire little suitcase full of presents for Marita; dolls that could be dressed and undressed, a horse with a yellow mane, a panda bear, dresses and shoes and comic books that were not to be found in Norway.

We were afraid that she wouldn't understand everything we said, Dixie said on the first evening after Synnøve and Kari had cleared the dinner table, when

Marita was exhausted and had fallen asleep in the arms of Grandpa Paul.

They thought it was a good idea that Johnny spoke English with the girl.

He was praised for it.

*

Paul and Dixie had to see a little bit of Norway since they had come all the way from New Jersey. Sigurd felt it was only right, and the first week they polished off what Sigurd called 'the compulsory': The Kon-Tiki Museum, the Viking Ships, Holmekollen Ski Jump, Akershus Fortress; even Ylva and Gunnar went along on the Saturday outing to Drøbak, where Sigurd had arranged a private guided tour followed by lunch at the Oscarsborg Castle.

The Norwegian grandparents felt that Paul and Dixie spoilt the little girl and they tried to let them know that it was not usual for Norwegian children to have sweets every day. Or soda pop. That only on rare occasions were they allowed to have such quantities of ice cream, pretty much only on the national holiday, the 17th of May. But Paul had snorted and said that he intended to buy whatever he wanted for Marita.

As long as we're visiting, he said, she's going to get exactly what she wants.

They travelled over the mountains on the Bergen Line. In Bergen, Paul carried Marita on his arm the whole time, even when they were just strolling around the city and she could have easily walked on her own. The plan was that after a few days in Bergen they would continue travelling, south along the coast, over to the towns of Stord, Bømlo and later to Stavanger, but before they reached Os, Paul's arm was hurting so much that they had to turn around to find a doctor in Bergen. It turned out to be tendonitis in his elbow, and he had to have a cortisone injection to relieve the pain. But he thought that was fine. He laughed and joked it off. He said to Marita with mock severity: Look what you've done to my arm, young lady.

She liked being called that.

Young lady.

Johnny watched his father from a distance, a few steps behind him across the square, from the other side of the table in the hotel restaurant where they had dinner. Paul sat with the little girl on his lap and she told him about the dolls she had brought with her to the restaurant.

This one here is Molly, Marita said. And this one here is named Candy because she is so sweet. This one is named Dumpappen.

That's a strange name, Paul said.

Doompaa-pn, he said.

No, Marita said and laughed. Mummy! Listen to Grandpa Paul!

Doompaa-pn, Paul said again. *Doompaa-pn*.

She unpacked her drawings and told her grandfather what the drawings were supposed to be.

This is New York, she said.

This is you working at the factory.

Here's Grandma Dixie in the kitchen making pancakes.

Here the two of you are sitting on the aeroplane from America. Can you draw on the plane?

Of course you can, Paul said. You can do all kinds of things on the plane.

Really?

Really.

It's just like . . . yes, just like a big ship, Paul said.

Mummy! Marita said, Grandpa Paul says that an aeroplane is just like a big ship!

That's right, it is, Kari said and smiled. She was trying. If she just kept smiling, it would all be fine. She was sure of it. She did her best, tried talking simply and easily with her in-laws but it felt as if the words got all tangled up. She sat with her head against the window of the train, watching the landscape rush past, like a child's drawing all stretched out. Looking out at the city from Fløien Mountain, her face white and shiny like a mask.

And her smile, Dixie later said to her husband. As if there were miles between the inside and the outside of the poor woman.

Johnny stroked Kari's arm, her back, her hair.

She tried. She dressed up, put on make-up. She had let her hair grow out and Dixie said that she looked well, that the hairstyle suited her, that she had put on some weight, but that it did her good.

But nobody was convinced by her tone of voice.

Everyone talked strangely this summer, Johnny thought.

Everyone except for Marita.

When they got back to Oslo, both Paul and Dixie were tired of the all bland food they were being served. Paul was not particularly fond of fish and Dixie, for her part, could not think of anything more boring than boiled potatoes. But they had given no sign of this and they had tried the salty fish soups, the cod and even the potato dumplings Sigurd had insisted on ordering at the hotel in Bergen. Back in Bygdøy they were invited to the home of a couple who were friends of Sigurd and Synnøve, where they were served a dish with broccoli. The conversation was forced and halting. During dinner, Paul said bluntly that he was not especially impressed by Norwegian food, shoved the vegetables over to the edge of his plate and said that he would prefer not to eat 'those little trees'. The next day Dixie occupied the kitchen. Now it was her turn to spoil them, she said. She had brought along cheddar cheese and buffalo-wing sauce from the US and on the days that followed she made pancakes, hamburgers, fried chicken and chocolate-chip cookies. Marita was over the moon and so was Johnny. But Sigurd reacted by developing a violent case of diarrhoea and Synnøve had to ask Dixie not to go near the kitchen any more. Paul thought it was all just foolishness, that Sigurd's unfortunate condition could not possibly be due to the food. But Johnny managed to convince his mother not to make a big deal out of it and accept that they were in fact staying in Sigurd and Synnøve's home and that it was only right that the host should personally decide what kind of food would be served.

When in Rome, Johnny said.

Yeah, well, at least those Romans knew how to cook, Paul said. Like your mother here.

Johnny's father-in-law got on his nerves more and more. He had got into the habit of calling whenever it suited him. It was usually about work and he therefore expected Johnny to jump on the first tram and be at his beck and call at all times. He also insisted on speaking Norwegian and Johnny had to fumble and search for words and sounds that he could not stand hearing himself pronounce.

Johnny hung up the phone. Put on his jacket and mittens. Tied the laces of his big, stupid shoes and went out to catch the tram. He got off at the National Theatre and walked the rest of the way up to Sigurd's office. The receptionist said something about a meeting that was almost finished, Johnny could just sit and wait if he liked. After a few minutes his father-in-law came out into the lobby wearing his hat and with his winter coat under his arm.

Let's go out, he said. I need to get some air.

They sat in the bar of the Bristol Hotel, where his father-in-law treated him to coffee and cake.

I have money, Sigurd, Johnny said.

His father-in-law nodded as if to a child. Never mind. Eat up, eat up, he said.

First, Johnny had to hear about constitution committees and party business.

He nodded. Said that he agreed.

Gas pipelines and the Soviet Union. The Energy Conference in Washington. The fishery border negotiations. Protection of the planned installations on the continental shelf.

His father-in-law stared out into space and searched for the right words, clearly satisfied.

Johnny was only able to follow in part, but nonetheless appeared attentive. Once in a while he asked about the meaning of a word or phrase, mostly to show that he was paying attention. What does *unnselig* mean? What does *uvegerlig* mean?

Later, his father-in-law gave Johnny a brown envelope.

Johnny accepted it without opening it.

Don't put too much work into it, his father-in-law said. It's for internal use only. Can you look through it by next week?

I can manage that, Johnny said.

Good.

Sigurd wiped his hands on the cloth napkin and drank up his coffee.

Johnny leant back on the sofa. If nothing else, he thought, it's nice and warm in here.

Well now, will you look at the time! his father-in-law said suddenly. Is it that late already? I have to run, Johnny. Say hi to the girls! he said, got to his feet, put on his hat and trotted out into the snow.

Johnny sat at the Bristol for a little while longer. Then he walked down towards Stortorvet Square. It was so quiet. The trams like enormous blue fishes across the white carpet of snow downtown. The snowflakes floated lazily down from the sky, grey and slow. He walked around the bend at Kirkeristen and looked at the clock. He had nothing to do. He decided that he wanted to walk out to the Akershus Fortress. Look at the fjord. The boats, like toys, down by the quay. The city was white and silent, and soon darkness would fall. He could tell by the sky. It was on its way. Hell, if it ain't like living in damn Wisconsin, he thought. Before taking the tram home he sat down at a coffee shop and leafed through the papers his father-in-law had given him.

He was so fed up.

He stuffed it all back into the envelope again.

He looked up at the sky. It was completely black out there now.

In the mailbox he found a letter from Billy.

Dinner's almost ready, Kari said when he walked in the door. Why are you so late?

She had made dinner. Marita was sitting in her room drawing.

Lovely, he said when he came into the kitchen. I'm starving to death. I met your father, by the way.

Yeah? What did he have to say? Complained about something or other, I guess.

Not really, Johnny said. Or, well, yes. He talked about the European Community again, about Vietnam and the party and the Soviet Union, you know.

God, Kari said. I don't know why he bothers. My mother is about to lose her mind with him. I can see it.

He's just interested, Johnny said. But he thought the same thing. That his father-in-law was nagging them all to death with all his knowledge and big words and political analyses.

Did things go well at work for you then? he said.

I'm sick of it, she said. It's boring. I don't want to talk about it. Come on now, eat. I'm not sure if it turned out OK.

Sure it did, he said. It looks good, anyway.

Marita! Kari called out suddenly and Johnny jumped. I'm not going to say it again! Dinner's on the table! Her voice was hoarse, she started to cough and her face turned red. Didn't you hear me calling or what? Kari said in irritation when Marita finally came in and sat down.

She's here now, Johnny said. Relax. Come on.

They ate in silence. The sound of forks and knives. In the hallway they heard the neighbours come home and let themselves into their flats. Marita asked if she could have more squash and Johnny got up from the table and mixed it.

Don't make it so strong, Kari said. You always make it so strong.

I got a letter from Billy today, Johnny said.

113

Kari smiled absently. How nice, she said, but as if she could have said just about anything.

From Uncle Billy? Marita said.

Yes, Johnny said.

He's not really your uncle, Kari said.

They fell silent. Afterwards they continued to eat and talked about other things. Kari did not say too much or too little and that was fine in a way. Marita was allowed to go to her room and Johnny helped with the dishes.

That was good, he said.

OK, she said.

It was.

OK, she repeated.

What is it with you, anyway?' Johnny asked.

With me? Nothing. What is it with you? Kari asked.

It stopped there.

Billy wrote that not long ago he had run into Paul and Dixie in Manhattan, completely by chance, that the whole damn war thing was totally fucked up and that he was glad that he was an old fool who didn't have to go off to some damn Asian country to be shot to pieces. New Jersey is the same old hole, by the way, he wrote. The same shit place as always.

When Johnny finished reading, he put a Sonny Rollins record on the turntable and lit a cigarette, but before the first track was over Kari came storming through the door.

Can you please turn that down? she said. I can't stand to be in the living room.

I have the volume on two, he said.

Makes no difference. I can't sit out there if the music's that loud.

Good God, Kari. The volume is on two! Johnny said again. But by then she had already turned around and closed the door.

He turned down the volume. But now it was so low that there was no point. He turned off the record player. Tossed the record back into the cover and read the letter from Billy one more time before putting it in a shoebox along with the others. He wished that he could just reach out his arm and touch her. That it could all be as simple as that. She slid away from him taking her beauty with her. Sometimes he thought about his life as a sacrifice, a kind of payback. He thought about the pain and how he would manage to bear the pain. He was always cold. He put on mittens and a hat and a scarf. He tried, at least. He pulled himself together, on a regular basis he tried to learn more words in Norwegian, words that he pronounced with a ridiculous, heavy accent that everyone smiled at. And even though they didn't mean any harm, he couldn't bear such looks.

He would like to live.

Kari looked at him with empty eyes.

Kari would also like to live.

They were like two mirrors.

One day Johnny found an envelope from The American Coordinating Council of Norway in the mailbox. An invitation. Welcoming him and his family to a Fourth of July celebration with his fellow countrymen in Frogner Park.

He mentioned it to Kari, but she didn't want to go.

It's not my independence day, she said.

Well, 17 May is not *my* independence day either, Johnny said. But I still celebrate it.

But you live here, she said. Is there something wrong with you? Besides, what's the point of celebrating the Fourth of July on 28 June? That's just stupid.

The Fourth of July isn't until the next Thursday, he said. People have to work, you know.

Whatever. I don't care anyway. Why are you carrying on about it like this?

I'm not carrying on, he said. I just thought we could go, all three of us, like a family.

She looked at him, but said nothing.

Anyway, I'm going, he said after a moment. With Marita.

So go then, Kari said. Her voice was completely flat.

And that was it.

The Fourth of July celebration was held near the Lincoln monument in Vigeland Park. When Marita and Johnny arrived, walking hand in hand, they were welcomed by a man from the Norwegian Worldwide Organisation. Marita said hello politely and introduced herself when the man reached out his hand and leant down towards her.

Welcome, welcome, welcome. The family entertainment will be starting any minute now, he said and pointed towards a tent. He opened a leather-bound notebook and wrote down Johnny's and Marita's names.

We like to know who's participating, he said.

Can I go see? Marita asked and looked up at Johnny.

Go ahead, he said. I'll be right there.

Is this your first time here?

Yes, Johnny said. It is.

And the mother? the man said.

She's Norwegian.

Oh.

She's not feeling very well, Johnny said. Has a cold.

Right, right. Let me see.

The man closed the book and pointed over towards the food tent. He mentioned a magician from Santa Fe who had been living in Løten since 1945. He came to Oslo every year for the specific purpose of providing entertainment.

How long have you been living in Norway? the man asked.

Since '67, Johnny said. My wife wanted to come home. You know.

Women, the man said. Can't live with them, can't live without them, right? He winked and slapped Johnny lightly on the back. Go on now, he said. Enjoy.

The magician was chalk-like, white and thin as a pencil. Marita stood on a chair and watched him pull rabbits out of a hat, make coins disappear, only to find them again behind the ears of the children.

Did you like it? Johnny asked when the magician had finished.

Yes! she said. He was very good.

They stood there waiting. A small woman emerged from behind a curtain and introduced two young girls who were about to perform a dance. Afterwards they were all told that the food tent was open, and Johnny

119

was served the best hamburger he could remember having had in years.

Oh, now we're talking, he said to the small group of people he was sitting with. It's not exactly easy finding a decent burger in this country. Where are you from?

They told him that they had come all the way from North Dakota, and that only one of them had been to Norway before.

New Jersey, he said when they asked him in turn.

What brought you here? they said.

Oh, you know, he said. And you? On holiday?

They explained that the Lincoln monument in the park had been a gift from the population of North Dakota to Norway.

Oh? When was that? Johnny asked.

In 1914, one of the men said. When Norway celebrated the 100-year anniversary of its constitution. There was a big centennial exhibition here.

We got a pretty strong Norwegian population, one of the ladies said.

I know, Johnny said.

Anyway, the man continued. Back then a big delegation came from North Dakota. Even Governor Louis B. Hanna was here. You know who that is?

Nope.

They told him a long story.

Marita came over to the table and asked if she could have a hamburger.

Of course you can, Johnny said and winked at the others.

And a Coke? she said, acting all cute and the North Dakota people laughed.

Of course, kid. After all, it's the Fourth of July, Johnny said.

You're right about that, they said.

Marita sat down with them and ate, before leaping up again and continuing to run around in the park with the other children and a little white dog.

Some of us are descendants of the 1914 delegation, one of the men said proudly. I am, and him and him and her.

What? Johnny said, having lost the thread.

Some of our grandparents were here for the unveiling, they said and pointed at the bust of Lincoln.

Oh. Yeah. Sure, Johnny said before the Kampen Veterans Marching Band, completely out of the blue, started up a horrific recital.

When the band was finished, Johnny excused himself and walked towards the booths where they were selling handicrafts.

He talked with the salespeople. Where you from? How long have you lived in Norway? What brought you here? Keeping an eye on Marita. She was sitting up against a tree and petting the white dog. More and more people arrived. A man carrying a megaphone walked around and informed them that they needed more players for the football game. They would be given helmets and equipment. A group of women marched past singing God Bless America. He bought an ice cream. He walked over to a small booth where they were selling spare ribs and hot dogs. On a platform right beside it a band stood playing in the scorching sunlight.

Never mind the sun, folks, just picture yourselves in a smoky club, you know, somewhere around . . . well, *anywhere* really. Anywhere in that great country of ours, the singer said.

Johnny stood there, listening to the band. A slow blues, the music rocked back and forth like a pendulum just before it stopped. People came and went. An elderly married couple sat down on a couple of plastic chairs beside him.

They're good, the man said. We saw them last year too.

Johnny nodded, Marita in the corner of his eye. The song ended and the singer mopped his forehead with a towel. 'I Wish I Was A Mole In The Ground'. 'When That Great Ship Went Down'. 'I Want to Be Like Jesus In My Heart'.

During intermission Johnny went over to the singer and thanked him for the music.

Thank you, the singer said. This is the second year we're doing this, I'm Marty, by the way, he said. You having a good time?

Yes, Johnny said. It's nice, this here. It's the first time I've come. My daughter and I. He pointed over towards Marita. Where you from?

I have a kind of base here in Oslo, Marty said. But I'm from St Louis.

Is that right? Johnny said. My father was in the army in St Louis.

Small world, Marty said.

Well, not *really*, Johnny said and laughed.

You're right, Marty said. You're right. Listen, I need to eat something before we go on again. A little food and a beer. Have you tried the barbecued chicken?

Johnny said that he had already eaten but asked whether Marty would like some company.

Sure, Marty said. Come on.

New Jersey? Marty said after having sat down with his food. You heard that new kid, Springsteen?

No, Johnny said.

From your neck of the woods, Marty said. Pretty soulful stuff. Young guy. Only 20-something. Very powerful.

The others in the band came over as well and sat down.

These are my bandits, Marty said. Henrik, the bass player, was from Tynset, Robert, the pianist, from Skedsmokorset.

They never let me down. Strange how a couple of white-breads can get it swingin' so goddamn good.

The boy who played the drums said nothing.

It was great, Johnny said. You sounded really good.

Henrik and Robert nodded with their mouths full. Thanks they said, almost in unison.

Marty glanced over his shoulder. Playing here is a little bit of, what can I say, a mixed blessing in a way. What's good is that the pay is decent at least. What's not so good, he said, is that people generally couldn't give a damn about what we're doing up there.

Or they ask if we can do *one they know*, Henrik said.

Don't get me started, Marty said.

You said you got a kind of base here? Johnny said.

Yup. I've got a crib in Bjølsen, where we live during the entire summer season. Me and C, Marty said, and only then did Johnny notice that the drummer was not a young man but a young girl.

Cindy's my kid, Marty said. She's been my buskin' companion since she was a little girl. Ain't that right, C?

Cindy nodded. She looked a little annoyed.

And you? Marty said. Why Norway?

For a moment he thought about telling it like it was. He would probably never meet these people again.

But he answered the way he usually did.

My wife wanted to come home, he said. She's Norwegian. I came with her because she wanted to be close to her family. How about you?

Long story, Marty said. I went to London with a band in the end of '65. Things with Olivia, Cindy's mum, had gone all to hell and I was desperate to get away from it all. I was tired of playing for rednecks who didn't do anything but throw beer bottles at the chicken wire. And, at that time, it was in England that it was happening, right? I had met a guy, Peter Grant, in Austin in 1963, right after Kennedy, I met him at a shitty bar where he played better than everybody else. He was a little older than me. Damn good. One of those musicians who talks through their horn. He was good with the audience too. So we started playing together. Our own stuff and some other things, old things, Blues mostly, Jimmy Reed, Howlin' Wolf, John Lee Hooker, all that stuff that the Stones were doing over in England. The same people. Peter really believed in what we were doing. And he had a devilish charm. He made you believe in yourself, that's the kind of guy he was. Strange, how it turned out in the end. Anyway.

We went to London. C was a little girl and I made a decision. I took her out of school and brought her along. In London we found ourselves a hell of a rhythm section, a wicked pianist and we started getting lots of jobs. We got some publicity too. People came to see us. Once we even got drunk with Neil Aspinall.

Who's that? Johnny said.

He was head of PR for The Beatles, Marty said. A childhood friend of Harrison and McCartney.

Oh, Johnny said. I'm not that familiar with The Beatles.

No, no. Anyway, Marty said. Everything went fine, for a while. Everything was peachy till Hendrix came to town and we saw him play and that was that. Peter, who was pretty much a drunk *already*, he fell apart. He couldn't get the hell over Jimi. And I understand him. Jimi was unreal. He was like from another planet. Had I been a more ambitious guy, I would have given up too.

He looked at Cindy.

And this one here, Marty said, hugging her to him. She's damn well been along for the whole ride. Every single little turn in the road, right, C?

Cindy nodded and smiled at Johnny.

And one of those turns brought me to Rome, where a soul band I was in was going to play for a few weeks.

But it fell apart and I didn't have no choice but to unpack my guitar and start playing on the street. We had no money. We had nowhere to live. We had no food. We met a load of people there who worked on the streets. Singers, actors, tightrope walkers. They told us we should travel south for the winter. Barcelona. Marrakech, places like that. And north for the summer. Denmark, Sweden, Norway. There was money to be made up there, they said. And so there was.

You still doing that? Johnny said.

Yeah, Marty said. But not as much as before. A little. When we get the itch, then we take off.

Sounds like a good plan, Johnny said.

That's right. It's not easy to give it up. C is trying to go to school some now, Marty said. To catch up . . . That's why . . . we're not as free as we used to be, let me just put it like that. He looked at his daughter. Even though I tried to teach her everything, she needs a little schooling. Right, C?

I guess, Cindy said.

Johnny said he wouldn't mind taking off once in a while. That he liked Oslo, but that the weather, especially the winters, he said, wore him down. They got tougher and tougher.

I know what you mean, Marty said and smiled. It gets dark and closes in on you and you sit here and long for home, right?

127

Johnny smiled back. Yeah, I guess I do. Sort of.

Tell me about it. It runs in our blood, Marty said after a long pause.

What does? Johnny said.

Missing stuff. All that runs in our blood. To stretch the leash as much as you can, right. Then be like a stray dog. To transform yourself into something unrecognizable, to burn up all the old stuff and make the most unreasonable demand—that all possibilities must be within reach. Am I right?

Johnny looked over at Cindy uncertainly, said he didn't know what he meant.

Sure you do, Marty said. You know. We learn the past by heart, the same past we had to kill to put up with this pandemonium of possibilities.

Again Johnny said that he didn't know. That he didn't understand, but it wasn't true.

America is full of slaves and fortune hunters, Marty said, full of con artists and adventurers. The ambitious. The greedy. That's who we are. All those who are given new names, who give themselves new names and become invisible against the horizon. The most effective mask, you know, is the one that is see-through.

Dad! Cindy said, and acted the way children do when they hear their parents repeat themselves for the hundredth time. Come on!

All right, all right, Marty said. I'll shut up. But the music, Marty said watching nobody in particular, the music allows us to look those possibilities right in the eye. Through music we can say anything. With any voice. That's what I mean. No matter how old the *singer* is, Marty said, he's never older than the song.

Marita was still playing with the white dog. She has sure grown over the past few months. Johnny waved and she waved a paper flag back at him. Breathless, she came running over to them and said: Daddy, Daddy, and Marty said: She's beautiful, and Cindy asked: Is she your only one?

On the street Dronningensgate, there is a run-down, second-hand shop where you can buy magazines— porn, mostly—and used records. Johnny is looking for three songs that Marty and the band played in Frogner Park. 'The Wagoners Lad', 'Last Fair Deal Gone Down' and 'The Lone Pilgrim'. He comes out of the store with a Doc Watson LP, but when he puts it on at home and listens to the first song, he is unable to concentrate on anything but a nasal woman's voice that he can't stand. He turns it off almost immediately. It was clearly something else he'd been looking for. This was hillbilly music. Sticky and sentimental and horrible.

A couple of weeks after the Fourth of July celebration, he meets Marty and Cindy again. Or, more precisely, he sees them playing on Karl Johan. It is a beautiful day, light blue, windless. Johnny has nothing to do. Marita is with Ylva, Kari in Bygdøy visiting her parents. He tosses a few coins into Cindy's hat and afterwards he goes with them to their place in Bjølsen for dinner. After they eat, Cindy goes out to meet friends, and Marty opens a bottle of wine.

He says Johnny has to give Doc Watson a chance, don't be fooled, he says. You have to get past all the trappings, everything you think you're hearing. It happens on the inside. You need to find some sort of combination first, a code that lets you in. He gets up, pulls out an LP and puts it on. Every time Johnny is about to say something, Marty shushes him and says: Just listen.

The sun sets behind the window sill.

Marty refills their glasses, and then plays the flip side.

Will you just listen to this?

But Johnny is not convinced. This summer's gone so damn slow, he says halfway through one of Doc Watson's songs.

Can't do shit about that, Marty says.

I hear you, Johnny says and brushes his fingers across the strings of Marty's acoustic guitar. Play me something, man, he says. Something *edgy*.

Marty pulls out a Robert Johnson recording. How about this one here, he says.

Robert Johnson is something else. The rough sound seems to come from a place Johnny recognizes, a place that emerges and disappears, as if he were constantly on the wrong hilltop.

Marty speaks with an admirable ease. Robert Johnson is a tangle of contradictions, he says. He's sad and he's funny. Optimistic and fatalistic. Dark and light. If you ask me, he sounds *innocent* and I'm not talking about lost innocence, I'm talking about the kind of innocence you give up voluntarily, and that you still remember afterwards and that burns like hell. Listen to it again, Marty says and allows Robert Johnson yet another turn on the record player. Listen to that wounded voice of his, hear how it cuts through time! When I listen to this, I feel almost a physical presence. Many people claim that he is overrated but I don't think so. Many people think Son House, or Charlie Patton, but not me. No fucking way. None of them can get so deep inside me. They might be more original, that's possible. You know, Keith Richards insists he can hear *two* guitar players and not one on Robert Johnson's recordings?

Pretty scary stuff, you know, considering . . .

Somewhere or other out there in the darkness a devil-dog with three heads is waiting. The rain is hammering down with biblical force, hail falling like stones from the heavens. A landscape also emerges: plains, mountains, New York in the spring, flags waving and Baptist churches, the faces of Kennedy and Nixon and Elvis; hillbillies without teeth, swaying choirs of black people and an intersection where the devil usually shows up. A sharply dressed gentleman. Johnny closes his eyes. I'm not sleeping, he says, and Marty answers, I know. Transformations, all kinds, a cheerful, polite

132

teenager, girls lifting up their dresses, young boys in uniforms, life guards, cowboys, jailbirds.

Play more, Johnny says. And pass me another cigarette.

Marty walks back and forth between the record player and the shelf. Johnny sits, half lies in his chair, looking at the cover photographs through thick blue smoke. Innocence, Johnny says absently, and then, as if he had suddenly returned from a deep forest: Fuck, Marty. This is so good.

It is just after nine o'clock. Johnny drinks coffee and leafs distractedly through the newspaper *Aftenposten*. The light arrives so slowly. Clouds drifting over Bekkelaget. Kari has left the radio on. The singing, child-like intonation. The Norwegian language from a distance. He shivers, goes into the bedroom to find a pair of wool ragg socks. Kari's clothes all over the bed. Dirty trousers and shirts on top of the dresser. Bed linens hung up to dry on the closet doors. He doesn't start work until fourth period today. He has time for another cup of coffee. He gets up, puts on his shoes and stands there as if paralysed.

A kind of blindness.

He knows there's something he isn't seeing.

Something he can't quite see.

He has to go home.

He simply has to take a trip back home, he says that afternoon when Kari comes home from work. He says he's constantly imagining things. Little films playing in his head. Films about ghosts and prairies and mountain chains and lakes. A kind of fire that's burning, a fire that for him *is* America.

It's hard to explain, he says.

Kari asks him if he can help put the groceries into the fridge. Says that she, in any case, can manage just fine without going back.

Ever? Johnny asks.

Kari says she doesn't know.

That she can't answer that.

But he has to go home. And he has to have money and they don't have any money. He always tries to say no when Dixie offers to send some. He knows that Paul is standing in the shadows and holding out his banknotes to him. An eternal reminder of who he was, who he could have been had things been different. Paul's money, his parents' class affiliation, *their place in the world*. And Johnny's downfall, into this servant-like existence so far away from home. His father-in-law's money, which Kari and he accept, which every single day reminds him that he lives in a borrowed country, a borrowed flat. He has learnt his father-in-law's requirements. He is obedient in this sense. The gratitude has become a burn mark.

In a newspaper he reads that the Müller Hotel in Mastemyr is looking for cleaning staff. Fuck it, he thinks. I can wash floors if that's what it takes. Better than asking my father for money. Better than crawling to Sigurd to ask for a loan. It's enough. I can clean toilets. He walks down to the main road, Mosseveien, takes a bus heading to Tårnåsen. At the reception he gives his name and is asked to wait. After a while a woman comes out, greets him and asks Johnny to follow her. She has short hair, like a boy. Johnny walks behind her, up a flight of stairs and through a large dining room where the woman says something that he doesn't quite catch. In her office he is offered coffee and even before he has sat down the woman has switched over to speaking English with him.

It's night work, she says, in the far wing of the hotel. What needs cleaning is the conference rooms, auditoriums, the bathrooms, the hallways and the reception areas. We have people who take care of the everyday cleaning. You won't have anything to do with that.

She speaks British English.

Every time she pronounces an *o* she exaggerates a bit and Johnny notices right away that she has nice eyes, a nice mouth. He tries to remember her name. He answers her questions. She talks about working hours and salary and her pronunciation gradually becomes broader—her *r*s are pushed further and further back into her mouth, the *a*s become more open and the *t*s softer.

This happens to him all the time. People who try to imitate his intonation.

You are the first person who has applied, says the woman. She sounds like she wants to be from Oklahoma.

He starts working at one o'clock in the morning, Fridays and Saturdays. First, he retrieves the cart from the broom closet, empties the rubbish in all of the rooms, ties the bags up together and throws them into the big bin bag before putting new bags in the rubbish bins. After that, he has to take care of the chairs, put them up on the tables so he can vacuum the soiled carpets. Broken, crumpled up plastic cups, damp napkins, fruit remnants, stems, chewing gum and mucus. Afterwards, he does the same thing in the rooms without carpets. Up with the chairs. Sweep up the rubbish, then vacuum clean, then wash the floors. Then he goes back to the broom closet and changes the water. Does the stairs, washes the hallways and the corridors and finally he cleans the enormous kitchen; washes counters, picks up leftover food, scrubs the sinks and stovetops and ovens and fans. Then the toilets last, that's the worst part, puts in new toilet paper rolls and scrubs away shit, piss and gobs of spit. Around 6 a.m. he makes himself some coffee, stands and yawns and looks out at the motorway. Collects all the gear, goes down to the laundry room and throws mop heads and rags into the washing machine. Hangs up his uniform. Locks doors, tries not to think too much. Around 7 a.m. he takes the bus home. Worn out and dead on his feet, he looks out across the Oslo Fjord, bathed in a blue, cold light. He takes out a little notebook and writes down the number of hours which he then multiplies by his hourly wage. Then he deducts taxes and enters the total in a separate column. He does this for the entire autumn. Every single weekend of the autumn of 1974.

But by January he can't take any more of the damn cleaning job. He's tired, worn out, and one morning he quits. The Norwegian Christmas party guests' Neanderthal-like behaviour has been feeding his aggression throughout the month of December. He can't fucking live like this. Chairs, walls, tables and toilets completely covered with vomit and blood and sperm and piss.

Enough is enough. Besides, the winter is dark and awful and it's been like that for months.

And Kari, she doesn't hardly speak at all.

In February, he tells her he will go by himself if she doesn't want to come along. He wants to scream at her that she can't hide.

But he doesn't know if it's true.

Maybe you can.

Maybe you can just forget everything, your whole damned life, leave it in a ditch and move on as if nothing has happened.

Once in a while, he tries to remind her of all the nice things, he talks about places that were once their places, back when everything was different, when they were other people, people who had not yet begun sinking down into this quagmire of a life that had been waiting for them. For one whole night they sat in the kitchen. At first the conversation resembles radio static, but the hours pass and Kari makes tea and Johnny says he loves her just like he used to do, he says that fate, that God, that he doesn't know why, that he doesn't know anything any longer either. She listens to him. Lights cigarette after cigarette. Watches him and looks at the darkness outside. She puts out her cigarette and starts to say something. She speaks so slowly, he lets her take the time she needs. She looks out the window and he thinks: What is she looking at? But he knows what. He knows what she sees and what she doesn't see. That time we took the America Line, she says, I was nauseous and dizzy. My mother had bought new dresses for Ylva and I, she says.

I felt like a princess.

She says it so slowly.

The night is dark blue, almost completely black. Johnny holds his cup with both hands. He says a thousand things and Kari looks at him and the kitchen slowly fills up with love, a love that crumbles, that will soon be mute and faint, but that remembers itself on this night.

I love you, he says and Kari sees Johnny Richards, those years by the shore, the years under the sun when their eyes didn't burn the way they do now.

But everything gets distorted. There is no way out.

He knows what she sees. He knows what she sees through that black window.

My God, Johnny says. I should have seen the girls too. Then you wouldn't be all alone with it.

Then they go to bed and afterwards sleep comes.

A dream about the garden, about the tree, where the girls are standing.

And then they fall inwards within the dream, as if through a shaft, towards something repulsive and sad, towards Kari who cries and cries beside her daughters.

And the girls.

Dressed in yellow dresses, ice-cream cones in their hands, alive and living.

And then Kari isn't able to cope with such dreams any more.

The future—sometimes a wall, sometimes a cloud.

She went to see a doctor her mother had recommended, who gave her pills. She started going to bed early, then started to oversleep. And when she finally got out of bed in the morning, her body felt as if it were cast in lead. She dragged herself into the bathroom and into the kitchen and, finally, to work.

But the pills helped. She never again dreamt about birds with black wings, she said.

What birds? Johnny said.

She didn't answer, but a few days later he asked again. They had just gone to bed.

Nothing, she said.

Why won't you tell me about the birds? he said. I want to hear about them.

Forget it, she said. Can't we just go to sleep? I've already taken my pill.

She rolled over and he lay there awake. Heard the snowplough in the distance. How it came closer.

You just have to shut your eyes and wait, he thought. Sooner or later sleep reaches you, like a hunter.

In the middle of the night he floated around and wove a landscape—Santa Monica and Long Beach. The white waves of childhood against the pier. A grey, almost white sky. A horizon that looked as if it had been drawn by hand. A pale green hotel. He stood and leant against a turquoise-coloured house in the middle of the day. It was light and warm. He saw motels and dives where the walls were covered with one graffiti drawing on top of the next. He dreamt of palm trees, merry-go-rounds and curved coastlines. He was suddenly 15, before him a mountain of pewter that did not budge an inch. Then yet another house, white as a shark. He dreamt of electric lights, arrows and signs. Taxis that turned into goldfish in a gigantic glass bowl that sooner or later would break. He dreamt about the New Jersey rain, about Tina Scott, about the shy American girls he drove home after having spent the day in the sun.

And he dreamt other dreams.

Harsh dreams that resembled gravel or mud; a burnt-down house, a house with a hole in it, like a jaw, a mine shaft leading straight to the gates of hell.

This is how spring comes.

The snow leaves behind enormous quantities of fine gravel and toy shovels and mittens. It trickles down from the rain gutters on the roof.

Johnny has just patched up Marita's bicycle. It's not dark. It's light. It's light and nice even though it is past seven.

Enough is enough, he says.

How can she shut everything up inside her?

But Kari won't talk about it. Maybe it is possible to hide.

Stop it, she says. Can you please lay off? What is it really that you want me to say?

He just wants her. Kari smiles a long and artificial smile, as if he'd just told a long story that didn't make any sense.

But he doesn't let go. He clings to these stammered conversations. Kari gets up, wants to leave, but Johnny follows after her.

No Kari, he says.

In the end she has to give in. She sits down again. Lights another cigarette and Johnny likes to believe that she appreciates his determination, in a way. Throughout the afternoon and the evening they talk. About Oslo and about his father-in-law and about Ylva and about the money they don't have.

And finally. Slowly. Carefully. Their names: Vera and Ann.

Vera and Ann.

And Marita.

It feels like the lash of a whip.

It's 5.30. It gets light. Johnny straightens his hair, wipes dried-out eyes.

You see? Kari says. But he doesn't know what she means.

You see, she says again as she gets up. Are you happy now?

Jesus, Kari. We can't just go around not talking to each other. That's all I'm trying to say.

You're out of your fucking mind, she says suddenly. The look she gives him. It's insane, he thinks. It seems as if she's about to howl, but she calms down.

I don't want to go back, she says. There's nothing for me there.

You have two daughters buried over there, he says. It comes out sharply, like an accusation.

I do *not*, Kari says. I have nothing over there, do you hear me? And this is the last time I'm going to say it, Johnny. Now you have to stop talking about it. I'm warning you.

Warning me? What is this? he says somewhat sarcastically, but what he says has no force. There is something inside him trembling with fear and she can see that. Smell it. She's like an animal.

Yes. I'm warning you, Johnny, Kari says. Her eyes are all white.

I'll fucking go alone if you don't want to come, he says after a while. With the same impotency.

I'll fucking take the kid and go alone.

It is a long summer. Perhaps the longest summer. Marita loves her grandparents' garden. She loves the beach her grandparents take her to and she loves ice cream and candyfloss and those apples with candy glaze that look good but are so sweet that she has to throw them away after just two or three bites. Grandma Dixie! she says, excited, ecstatic, and Grandma Dixie takes her around the neighbourhood and shows off the living grandchild and hardly thinks of Vera or Ann, because Grandma Dixie has packed up the photographs of the other girls and Grandpa Paul has hidden them out in the garage, in unmarked boxes on shelves he made and put up himself.

Johnny breathes in the smell of death. He knows he has to. He holds Marita's hand. When he meets old friends, they look at him with compassion. Love and grief, woven into each other. He wonders how it's even possible to stand such contradictions.

Billy comes by in his new car and Marita takes his hand as if she were a grown-up and says: Nice to meet you Uncle Billy and Billy says: Oh man, she's just heart-breakingly beautiful.

Marita gets in the back seat. Johnny sits beside Billy and they turn up the radio and Marita learns some songs that are popular that summer and Uncle Billy is so sweet and kind to her and he teaches her the lyrics of the songs they sing while the wind smells of the ocean and the sand and the enormous yellow sun drips on all of them.

Marita in a striped bathing suit, lying on a huge fuzzy towel Grandma Dixie bought for her.

There are no waves in Norway, Marita says. She and Grandma are out swimming in the ocean. There's no sand, either. There's just stones and grass. But it's still nice, though.

The summer is long, full of sunshine, and Marita walks around holding her father's hand, seeing things she's never seen before, things she'll never ever forget. Grandpa Paul lets her sit on his lap and steer the car back and forth on the street where they live. Grandma Dixie tells her stories about the family and, afterwards, when Johnny sits on the edge of her bed and asks Marita if she's had a nice day or if she wants him to read to her, Marita says: Can't Grandma Dixie come up and tell me a story? And Dixie dries her eyes and gets up from her television-watching chair and walks up the stairs and sits down by the bed and Marita says: And then what happened?

145

Do you know where the Ukraine is? Dixie says. She looks at her granddaughter, kind of summons her strength. Repeats stories she heard herself as a child. And the summer is long and full of stories. Johnny runs into the supermarket to buy food and drink. Uncle Billy tells stories while he and Marita are waiting in the car.

Did you know that your daddy was one of the best divers we've had here in New Jersey? Billy says.

No, Marita says. Is it true?

Just wait till we get out to Sandy Hook, Billy says. Just wait.

The Atlantic Ocean. They eat dinner at a family restaurant. They go swimming all afternoon and Johnny really dives like a film star.

Don't you think? Billy says.

Marita squints up towards the rock where her father is standing and waving and carrying on like a teenager, before he throws his body out and keeps his eyes open wide all the way down until he hits the water and sinks down into the green stillness.

When the sun goes down, they stay on the beach, sitting and watching the waves come closer and closer. Marita shivers and Johnny wraps her up in one of his old wool jumpers that he brought along. Afternoons, evenings, entire seasons on the inside the sleeves and the front and the knotty stitches. Vera and Ann. Vera and Ann. He looks out at the water. Wants to say something to Billy. But holds back.

What? Billy says.

Nothing, Johnny says. Forget about it.

Marita falls asleep in the back seat on the way home. Johnny and Billy don't say much, almost nothing. Once in a while they look at each other and smile and one of them says, maybe: It's so good to see you, man.

When they reach Freehold, Johnny carries the sleeping child out of the car and up the front steps of the house and all the way up to the bedroom, where Marita wakes up and twists and undresses slowly while she asks if Grandma Dixie can come up and continue the story.

I believe Grandma Dixie is a little busy right now, Johnny says.

Please, she says.

*

We met each other in New York, Dixie says.

They walk hand in hand towards the local supermarket. Your mother and father also met each other in New York. Maybe it's something that runs in the family, Dixie says and smiles. Did your father tell you about it?

No, Marita says.

You'll have to ask him, Dixie says. For a moment the girl smiles in a way that makes Dixie jump and then she gets all cold inside and has to stop and sit down on a bench for a minute to collect herself.

I just got a little warm, she says.

They cross the street and the car park and then they go into the supermarket.

At least it's nice and cool in here, Grandma says. She takes a shopping cart and asks if there's anything that Marita wants.

Chocolate milk, she says. Can I have that?

Yes, Dixie says. Of course you can.

Dad said we're going to New York maybe on Saturday, Marita says. What day is it today?

Today's Tuesday.

So four days to go.

That's right, Dixie says. You'll like the city. It's so nice! The best city in the world!

I can't wait, Marita says. But then what happened? You have to tell me!

They are on their way home with the shopping bags. Well, Dixie says. Grandpa Paul lived right by where my family lived. He was much older than me, she continues. I was just a little girl. For me he was a man. And I looked at him and he looked at me and one day we talked a bit. There was a little park where we used to sit in the afternoons, my girlfriends and I. And Grandpa Paul and his work buddies too. One day we girls stood there and talked to them and he said my name. Daria, he said. A few days later he talked me into bringing him along so he could talk to my father and ask permission to take me to Manhattan. He had figured out that I liked jazz. I was thrilled to pieces. I loved it. The music and the thick cigarette smoke that floated between us and then he called me Dixie and on the way home he took my hand and didn't let go of it until we'd come all the way to my door.

Sim sim sal abim, Dixie says as she puts the bags down on the kitchen counter.

And then you went steady, Marita says.

Yes, Dixie says. And afterwards, when we got married, we stayed in New York for a while, in the South Bronx. It was only after your father was born that we moved out here, when Paul began working at the textile factory.

The sun is up, the sky is blue, it's beautiful and so are you, Johnny sings in the morning when he wakes Marita up. She yawns and stretches like a cat. Grandma Dixie spoils them with pancakes and maple syrup and Johnny says Kari would go nuts if she knew how much sugar Marita was swallowing. Once a week he calls home to Norway, sits on the ottoman out in the hallway where the telephone is and dials the number. Kari sounds tired. Says she hasn't been doing anything special. The weather. That she's been to see Ylva. That the summer has been cold and grey, mostly. One evening Johnny calls and she is excited and giggly and he asks her if she's been drinking and Kari says *maybe* in a playful and girlish way. Johnny hears a remote resonance in her voice and says that it's only three in the afternoon over there and Kari replies, teasingly: *So?*

Johnny stays up, by himself in the living room, after everyone has gone to bed. The wind is rustling in the treetops; he turns on a light, a lamp his mother bought him when he was a child. There is a child in here who is him. Another ghost unable to find peace. He sees himself, with a new haircut, wearing shorts. In the kitchen, dipping cookies in warm milk that makes him queasy. He remembers the day his father comes home with a new car and they just drive around for hours. Paul has become so old. He walks so slowly and his eyes, it's as if they are paler now than they used to be. Coated with a shiny membrane. But he still goes to work, even though Dixie says his father no longer really has anything to do with daily operations. He has an office in there. He's not fooling anybody, Dixie says. He's not even fooling himself, but he doesn't know what else to do. You know your father.

But does he know his father?

He doesn't. Years have passed. What's there to know, really?

Sometimes they look at each other from across the dinner table but prefer to avoid each other's gaze. Johnny can see that Paul loves the little one. When Marita talks, something happens. To both of them. To all of them.

Johnny reaches over to the lamp, flicks off the switch. He sits there for a while in the semi-darkness, he should go to bed soon, but he doesn't move.

Billy picks him up in the evenings. Marita is in the living room with her grandparents, watching TV. She likes the commercials and learns all of the songs by heart. Johnny hears Billy honk, puts on his jacket and goes out. Bruce Springsteen, Billy says and holds up a cassette tape. Bruce Springsteen was born here too, in Freehold, and it's kind of fun that a rising star comes from the neighbourhood, more or less. Johnny agrees, mostly. But when he hears Springsteen's music, he's neither impressed nor particularly enthusiastic. There could be all kinds of explanations: Marita's questions, seeing his mother again, the almost intolerable polite-ness he and his father have replaced the arguments with. Maybe Johnny has enough on his hands this summer, just dealing with the distance, between the life he lives in Norway and the life he left behind in New Jersey.

He only half listens to the tape that Billy has put on. That's the truth.

But he doesn't give up, Billy, and in between all the other things they talk about this summer, he keeps coming back to Bruce Springsteen. He turns over the cassette. Again and again.

They drive somewhere. Park the car and drink beer. They meet old friends and try to repeat things that cannot be repeated. They both understand. But they don't know what else to do. They imitate themselves as best they can.

It will have to do.

It's a way of talking.

Billy wants a girlfriend, he says. His greatest fear in life is he'll end up lonely, without a woman. He is 35, he says. It's been nine years since things ended with Sylvia, his high-school sweetheart, the one who broke his heart so bad that Billy still thinks he loves her, and that's the reason why he is incapable of being in a relationship with anybody else.

Fuck, he says.

He orders another round, greets acquaintances and introduces Johnny to people. My best friend, Billy says. My oldest friend, Billy says. We go way, way back, Johnny says. They're like a chorus. Billy's acquaintances sit down at their table. When they find out that Johnny lives in Norway, they ask if Norway is in Europe and later they probe him with questions about Europe, if the women go topless and Johnny says they do, in the summertime. On the beach, anyway.

Jesus, Billy's buddies say. That must be totally insane.

Then they move on. Billy and Johnny. Put on their jackets and go out of one bar and into another.

Does the little one like it here, then? Billy asks. Johnny replies that she loves it. That he is so glad he brought her with him. And then Billy says: And Kari? How're things with Kari? And Johnny talks about Kari. And it helps.

It helps a little.

By the time he gets back to his parents' house, he has had a little too much to drink. Dixie is sitting in the living room with the television on, and the sound off.

What are you watching? Johnny asks.

Nothing, Dixie says. I just leave it on to keep me company.

And Dad?

He's asleep. Do you want something to eat? You want me to make you something? she asks.

No thanks, Johnny says. We had something to eat just a little while ago. Besides, I feel a little sick. Billy weaves when he drives. I think it made me a little carsick.

Dixie leans back on the couch and yawns. Well, maybe it's time to go to bed, she says.

Mom, Johnny says, suddenly, in a little-boy voice, with a fear on the tip of his tongue.

Yes? she says.

She looks like them doesn't she?

Dixie drops her gaze.

You mustn't think so much about that, son, she says. But her voices trembles. She can hear it, this won't do. So she adds: Nothing good will come of it. That's all I'm saying.

But she does, doesn't she?

Johnny . . . she says. He waits. But she says nothing more.

Answer me, he says, his voice is sharp. Just say it.

His mother looks at him for a long time. Yes, she does, she says finally. And then she smiles. But she is a unique little creature, Johnny. I am so fond of her. You should hear the things she says, everything she asks about.

I know, Johnny says. She asks questions all the time.

The light in the living room flickers and throws shadows back and forth from wall to wall, floor to ceiling, shadows standing in the tiny distance between Johnny and his mother.

Even when she sleeps, he says. She sleeps on her stomach, with her arm hanging down from the bed, just like the girls.

He wrings his hands. Sort of summons his strength.

Kari doesn't want us to tell her anything. You have no idea how many arguments we have had about it, he says. I think . . . I feel it's unfair, you know? Sooner or later she has to know. We can't keep it a secret for ever.

Maybe it's just because she's still too little, Dixie says. Maybe she won't understand.

Oh, please, Johnny says. Do *you* understand what it means, maybe? Do *I* understand it? The hell I do.

Calm down.

I don't understand shit. Don't you see? The only thing I understand is that I'm back here and that all I can see is the girls, everywhere, every single day, in every damn thing.

Calm down, Johnny, his mother says again.

But he keeps going.

I don't know what I'm supposed to do. She asks and asks and I answer her as best I can. But sooner or later . . . and Kari . . .

She's only six years old, Johnny, Dixie says. She's just a child. Think about what it could do to her. Maybe Kari is right, that it's not such a good idea, that maybe it's better to wait.

He is silent. On the screen there's a clown and it makes him smile.

Billy's afraid of becoming an old bachelor, he says.

Well, strictly speaking, he already is, Dixie says.

Yeah, well, Johnny says and smiles. I guess. But I didn't have the heart to tell him.

Dixie looks up at him.

Are you OK, son? she says, finally. I know it's not easy. I'm so happy to have you home. Both of you. We are happy, both of us. Paul and I.

That's good, Johnny says. It's good to be home. I want you to know that. He falls silent. It looks as if he is about to sit down, but he just stands there, fumbling with his jumper instead.

Have you told her the entire family history now? Johnny says. She wants you to come up and tuck her in every single night.

Yes, Dixie says. She is so lovely. I have told her about both sides of the family, yes. She thought that Ellis Island and the name changes and all of that was really exciting. She wanted to hear about it again and again.

Maybe I should take her on a little trip there.

Oh, she would enjoy that, Dixie says.

Yeah, Johnny says. We have to go in to Manhattan. Maybe this weekend. Do you have any plans this weekend?

Not that I know of, Dixie says. I don't know if your father has something planned or not.

He looks so old.

He's getting older, Dixie says. We all are.

Not you, Johnny says.

Stop it, his mother says, and smiles.

I mean it, he says. It's as if he has got heavier. He looks old.

He's 73 years old, Johnny. That's an entire lifetime.

But you . . .

That's enough, Dixie says abruptly. It'll be fine. You know your father.

But Johnny doesn't know if it will be fine.

I think I'll go to bed, Mum.

I'm going to sit up a little longer, Dixie says.

OK, Johnny says. Good night.

Come here, she says. Give me a kiss.

In New York, as they are sitting there, each holding a melting ice-cream cone, on a bench in Central Park, Johnny starts bawling in front of his little girl. When he feels the tears well up, he knows that it's all wrong. He tightens his jaw. Tries not to blink. Swallows and swallows, but it doesn't help. He can't stop. His mouth contorts, tightens, his lips begin to tremble. And then his eyes fill with tears and make everything misty. He doesn't have a chance, he has no strength left, his face transforms into an ugly, frightening grimace right before his daughter's eyes. She looks at him, says nothing. Johnny blinks, squeezes his eyes tightly shut, tears fall down onto his shirt, his hands on their way up to wipe them away. He doesn't know why, but it makes him even sadder; the sight of the wet spots on his clothes rips his face open and then he whimpers as quietly as he can, as if it would help, but it doesn't help. He shakes, sobs, tries to swallow the tears, push them back down into his gut, his intestines or wherever they come from. But the tears just well up. Disgusting sounds that don't belong to him, but to somebody else, something else.

When he finally catches his breath, he tells Marita everything, as carefully as he can. He feels something slip when he says the names Vera and Ann. He talks slowly, he looks for the right words and weighs them with the greatest care. At first he says nothing about the dangling head, nothing about Kari who one day goes to the morgue, and nothing about the bones and the tiny torn-up bodies that Kari thought she just had to see and that he didn't want to see. But Marita asks, and when Marita asks, it gives a little and Johnny takes deep breaths and he thinks that his little girl is also breathing deeply and she continues to ask and he notices his guard is down, no walls around him. Marita asks questions and Johnny shakes and sobs and she has no other choice but to be the child who comforts her father.

That's where we used to live, Johnny says a few days later, when they go to see the old house. Something breaks into pieces inside him and Marita is frightened at first and people come over to them and ask if something is wrong and Johnny stands in the middle of the street, nothing but a torn-up man and Marita has to answer, not letting go of his hand for anything in the world. The nice people look at Johnny, ask what's happening, if something has happened, if there is something they can do for him, for them.

It is Marita who answers.

It's OK. He's my dad, she says, and Johnny is able to breathe again when they start walking down the street, away from the house, away from the turn in the road, away from Mona and Terry who moved away too, and never wrote or called or anything.

Marita asking questions. Lying on her bed, asking. The patience of an animal. Johnny is silent for long stretches of time. And then he tries to talk, but it takes a while before he is able. But Marita asks. Then she waits and they go back to the house another day and this time it's better, even though Johnny has to bite his tongue to keep from starting up again, some hideous thing forms in his face, but the tears don't come, he doesn't break apart. Marita asks if they can go into the backyard but they can't do that, another family is living there now, Johnny says, and so they stand there for a while and look through the window. A car comes around the corner and Johnny says the name George Swensen and he knows it's too late to stop because Marita is looking at the backyard and in through the window where another family is living and Johnny's story ends up where it must end. When it's finished, he feels as if he has been run over by a freight train, but his little girl looks so strong, all of a sudden, when the nice adults from a few days before come walking across the street and Marita says hello to them and the adults stop and say: Hello, little girl, what's your name? and they look up at Johnny nervously and down at Marita again and they say: You're so beautiful, and Marita says she was born in Norway and the adults say: Do you like it here? and Marita answers: Yes, yes, yes. I love it here.

My sisters died here.

Home. Back home in Norway. He entered the flat, put down the suitcases by the hall closet, helped Marita take off the pretty coat that Grandma Dixie had given her. He felt awkward and unreasonable. Kari went into the living room to light the candles she had put out. She had baked, she said. She had set the living-room table, a red tablecloth and napkins. He saw Marita jump up onto a chair. She called to him from the living room, asked if she could start cutting the cake. Kari had made an effort.

He kissed his wife. The flat felt oddly unfamiliar, as if distant, removed from everything he'd grown accustomed to over the course of the summer: the language, the drives with Billy, the silence in the house and the kid's questions. He had hardly thought about the flat, about Bekkelaget, or his in-laws. He had thought about Kari, but it was another Kari he saw. The one from before the accident. The *American Kari*, he thought. Someone he had, at the time, imagined her to be.

It felt like a black hole. There were three of them, but around the table there were five.

A torn-up life.

Marita cutting slices of cake and serving, playing that she was serving. Reflections, the little white hand raising a glass, the hand reaching across the mouth and wiping away crumbs. The walls, the carpeted living room, the tiny distance between the bedroom and the bathroom, Kari's tablecloth and apple cake, a thermos of coffee—this too was Johnny's life.

It wasn't a bad life.

At Christmas time, Billy wrote him a long letter where he did nothing but rave about how unbelievably great Bruce Springsteen's newly released *Born to Run* album was. He had enclosed photocopies of two articles, one from *Time*, the other from *Newsweek*—and also a panegyrical review of a concert Bruce Springsteen had given in London earlier that autumn. Johnny decided to give Bruce Springsteen another chance. He bought *Born to Run* and read the articles, but had trouble understanding what all the fuss was about. He mentioned this to Marty one evening when they were out at Club 7, where the bass player Henrik was playing in a jazz trio as backup for a Norwegian poet whom Johnny didn't understand for shit. The music in itself was not bad, Johnny said to Marty, he especially liked when Springsteen verged on soul music. But Marty shook his head and lit a cigarette and said it was the stories. He's a good storyteller, he said. It's like he sits around the campfire and talks to you. That's how you have to listen to him. But Johnny wasn't sure. *He fills up his songs with way too many words*, Johnny wrote to Billy, after having played through *Born to Run* not only once but then two and then three times. *It's not just because I think that Dylan writes boring melodies that I don't like Dylan, you know*, he wrote, *but because Dylan, too, uses so many words. There's so much talking*!

And Springsteen, wasn't he exactly one of those *new Dylans*?

But Johnny never mailed the letter to Billy. One evening when he was at home alone (Kari and Marita were staying with Kari's parents—Johnny had begged off, claiming he had a headache) he sort of found his way into Springsteen's music for the first time. Especially 'Jungleland', the last song on the album, leapt towards him, as if tentacles emerged out of the dim light of the office and grabbed hold of him, grasping his wrists and throat and heart. While listening to the song Johnny began to envision things he never knew he needed to see, things that soothed him, that lay themselves over him like cool washcloths, just like when you lie racked with fever and hallucinations, and somebody comes in and sits down on the edge of your bed. Suddenly—as if without warning he had been given a puzzle with a thousand pieces and without any effort had put it together perfectly—he recognized Springsteen's universe. It resembled his life. When

Springsteen sang about 'the Magic Rat', Johnny thought about the Circus Dwarf, his buddy who had painted flames on the Dodge his father had given him for his 16th birthday. And right behind the Circus Dwarf's Dodge came a whole series of other glimpses: the barefoot girls sitting on the bonnet in the song and the barefoot girls from a time when Johnny was still *Johnny Boy Richards*, when entire afternoons were spent polishing the chrome mudguards of his father's Chevy, when Johnny still glided through those Friday evenings in his father's car, beer cans in a cooler in the boot.

The warm summer rain. The burger joints. The kosher delis.

The mom-and-pop shops and the future, like a promise of never-ending happiness.

He froze when he heard Springsteen sing 'over the Jersey state line', he could see the strange darkness within him settling over his home town. The autumn leaves hanging from the trees. His adolescence wrapped in melodies and phrases. It's like a damn mirror, he thought.

The kids around here are just like shadows.

Always quiet, holding hands.

Then he played 'Jungleland' again and turned the record over and he kept on doing this for a few months, before he went out and bought Springsteen's first two albums, which indeed were even more verbose than

Born To Run, but also—to an even greater extent—about New Jersey. *Greetings From Asbury Park* cut into his heart. The first time he heard the opening lines of 'The Angel' tears filled his eyes; the hunchback children and the angel who came down to New Jersey, who took the deformed bodies along up to heaven. *The Wild, the Innocent & the E Street Shuffle* made him laugh. That was the cassette Billy had played in the car. He recognized some of the songs. But they were different now. The same songs, but different songs. 'Billy's down on the railroad tracks,' Springsteen sang and Johnny exhaled as if he'd been under water for years, seeing his own Billy. He sat down and wrote a letter a mile long while he turned the record over and over and smiled into space like an idiot, but an idiot who didn't care, an idiot who is being watched while looking at something fabulous.

And he thought, I could cry now if I wanted to. If I go any further into this, I'll cry.

And he wrote that too, to Billy.

I love you, man, Johnny wrote, *and these songs make me miss all kinds of shit.*

*

From that day on he would sometimes wake up at night and remember dreams about amusement parks, lights and clouds that looked like candyfloss covering up the heavens. It was a kind of fear, like vertigo. Searching for a country. A place that waits for you even though you're long gone.

Even when you die, your country keeps waiting, Marty said. And in our case, Johnny, it's waiting beneath a sky crowned with vultures. How about that.

And Johnny remembered. When he sat down on Marty's couch and the turntable spun, he remembered the kinds of things that he liked remembering, and everything grew bigger, better. Once in a while he dreamt that the girls were still alive and that Marita was there too, under a huge parasol on the boardwalk in Asbury Park, where they all sat and drank lemonade from a glass that never went dry.

The biggest difference between the first two Springsteen albums and *Born to Run* was the people who populated them, Johnny wrote. Billy wasn't sure. He thought it mainly had to do with changes in the band, but then again, he'd seen The E Street Band a bunch of times over the past few years. Even though times are hard, you know, with the recession and all these demonstrations and the war and all that shit, Billy wrote, Asbury Park still comes to life at weekends.

I'm sitting on the other side of the globe staring at America, Johnny replied, and sometimes it feels like I manage to cut through this damn winter darkness, if I put on the right music, when I really need to think about something else besides how the light disappears at 3 p.m. Hell. I'm sinking deeper and deeper down into this shit, Billy. What was it we escaped? You think about that? Why were we the ones who got out of it? Of having to wade around in the Vietnamese jungle? I think about it a lot. About the kinds of jungles we escape from and the kinds of jungles we live in. Fuck. It was so good to be home last summer. And strange. Everything that's different and everything that's the same. I am so glad that you didn't stop going on and on about Springsteen. He has kept me in one piece the whole autumn. I know it has to do with me, but it feels as if *I* am everyone he sings about, that's how it feels. But don't you think there are fewer strange people in *Born to Run* than on the other records? Fewer, like, local characters? It's less humorous, but better.

You with me?

There were still magical nights, burning nights opening up, nights when the road could lead anywhere. Do we ever grow up? If so, how? If so, where do we leave our former *selves*? The record was full of wings, shiny hubcaps, red roses and *Love*—an aching incomprehensibility that held life together and tore it apart at the same time. It was still possible to get out. Out and away. And the insistence that everything was possible, that in America one could transform one's life into whatever it might be was seductively, romantically enshrouded in all those nightly threats: knife dramas, the mercurial reflection from the pavements, everything that came after daily life, *the working day*, was out of the way.

On *Born to Run* the dream is the only inhabitable place, Marty said, the only place where it's possible to endure the monotony of real life. Even the two characters in 'Meeting Across the River' cling to the promise—it will get better. It *can* get better. That's what the nation pounds into us, Johnny. If you haven't become the one you want to be, you just have to go west, right? That's where the open country is. The endless sky. That's where we can invent a new life. That's the promise.

The authority in these songs is so dramatic, Johnny wrote in a letter to Billy, one night when he had one beer too many.

It was not like him to talk that way.

They were Marty's words he used.

*

On his 37th birthday he got two albums in the mail, from Billy: Dylan's *Another Side of Bob Dylan* and *Highway 61*. But Johnny had a hard time swallowing them; both the acoustic and the electric surrealism were too much for him. Sometimes it was just nonsense, he thought, although there were two or three songs that stood out. But it wasn't until Marty played Jimi Hendrix's version of 'All Along the Watchtower' that Johnny began to understand Dylan's ragged qualities. After the Easter holiday (which he spent in Gol with the rest of the family) Johnny had a call from Marty. He and Cindy were back from southern Spain, from Istanbul and Greece and Italy, where they'd been all winter. They met in Bjølsen. They talked about Bob Dylan and Marty insisted that Johnny borrow *John Wesley Harding*. He taped it when he came home and it turned out to be an album that Johnny not only understood, but one that he played to pieces, almost; to Kari's despair, Dylan's harmonica seemed—during a four–five month period in 1976—to cut through the walls and the ceiling regardless of where in the flat she might be.

Is there anything worse? Kari said. Good lord!

And Johnny said: The trick is to listen to it the same way you listen to Miles.

I don't listen to Miles, she said.

When *Darkness on the Edge of Town* was released in 1978, Johnny was so deeply inside Bruce Springsteen's universe that it was almost impossible to disappoint him. Not that he feared being disappointed, to the contrary. He expected, like everybody else, a follow-up just as huge, visionary and haunting as *Born to Run*. But the follow-up was different in so many ways. A kind of flip side. The lovers were now running on empty. They'd become stuck within themselves, in their home town, the monotonous factory work or the equally monotonous unemployment. They had become middle-aged people now, people with children and houses far too small, people who were stuck in a swamp called daily life, a life called trying to make ends meet, called *we don't talk to each other any longer, Kari*.

What highways snake through his life?

What is his desert?

He thinks about swallowing all his pride and asking his father-in-law for a loan. He wants to buy a car. He talks Kari into it first, and then he asks his father-in-law and Sigurd agrees and before Johnny knows it, a blue Volvo is parked outside, a used one, but all the same a car that is more than good enough for them. Johnny says thanks, says they will of course pay for it. Sigurd says one of Gunnar's colleagues has been using the Volvo as a 'wife car' and Johnny has never heard the expression before and everything gets mixed up with the shame, the feeling of hanging by a thread, of being tied to a machine with teeth and gears. He sits behind the wheel and hunts for mirages, drives on the Mosseveien motorway out towards Vinterbro, even further, towards Ski, Ås, Drøbak. He smokes and drives and thinks about what it means—*To take the wheel*, it's called here in Norway. To do one's best to live right. To get up every morning and go to work every day. But the eyes go blind and the blood runs cold. To feel so weak that you just want to explode. To tear this city apart. Everything collapses into everything else. Do you want to come along for a drive? Out to Svartskog, down to the water. Why don't we take a knife and cut away the pain that grows around our hearts? Why don't we become the people we once were, just for tonight, just for tonight pretend as if something is going to start and not end.

I'm not a boy.

I'm a man.

A grown man who sees a dark cloud rising up from the desert floor.

This is how I talk.

But he had to be a ventriloquist, in Oslo he was a damn clown with a puppet of himself on his lap. Everything Norwegian stabbed him in the chest. Norwegians smiled such idiotic smiles when they were nervous. And this fucking smile is beginning to rub off on me, he thought. Every day, everything filled up with gazes that were evasive, that almost never met his own. People who looked as if they were afraid of other people. Damn peasants. That was why the music saved him. He needed someone to talk to, and that someone had to be America, his own nostalgic reflection, what Marty— when he had come far enough down in the bottle of wine—called *a complex construction*. The memory. The memories. What nobody could get inside of.

My shit.

When Johnny finally found these memories, when he finally managed to picture the afternoons and evenings and nights he so wanted to haunt, it all began flying away, like an arrow, at a hellish speed towards a house that once was theirs, towards a happiness that had once been there, towards the two who were now a maimed shadow, destroyed children who slunk along the walls of life. While Johnny listens to the music, all those beautiful glimpses are suddenly tangled up in the horror of the present, in its shrill din, and then, then everything is broken.

*

One day he heard Simon & Garfunkel's 'Bridge over Troubled Water' on the radio, a song that he until then thought was intolerably sappy. And it could have been the day, it could have been him, it could have been a million things. He went down to the city centre the next day, it was a Saturday and he took Marita with him. He bought records with money he didn't really have. Simon & Garfunkel. The Doors. Neil Young. He wrapped himself up in the songs, on the inside he built something; his grief and sadness found places to live. In the songs he placed his own pathetic character— Johnny Richards in the middle of Simon & Garfunkel's 'America'. Johnny and Kari, who in the song was named Kathy, but it was her and it was her as Kari had once been, young, full of lust for life and laughter and her eyes that had long ago stopped looking at him in any way whatsoever. Johnny and Kari who buy a pack of cigarettes and pies from Mrs Wagner. Johnny and Kari walking down the street, on a highway, standing at a petrol station in the middle of nowhere, in a desert, in a silence that's not to be found anywhere except in this misleading musical glimpse. Isn't it easy to imagine things? Another life? A fate other than this one? A place where he helps her with her suitcase, where he and Kari board a Greyhound in Pittsburgh, where she sits by the window so she can see the road, the drizzle, the past. Michigan seems like a dream to me now, Johnny says, and then they laugh while the bus glides through America, while an old woman shushes them several times when they talk too loud, when they laugh too loud, when it's the sounds of being in love that are heard. But they don't care. They've gone to look for America. They want to find America, which in the song is the same as them, as Johnny and Kari, the same landscape, something enormous and open and free. Something created for the future to inhabit.

Later that same evening, after they've got off the bus and checked into a cheap motel by the highway, they lie on their backs on the narrow, hard bed. Johnny says: The bedspread smells like shit; and Kari says: Toss me a cigarette, I think there's one in my raincoat.

We smoked the last one an hour ago, he says.

It could have ended there.

In America.

Halfway through a song that Johnny never thought he'd like. It could have ended with the two of them, the young couple in love on a dirty bed in America. But it doesn't and for the last verse Johnny has to close his eyes while he listens to the words:

    'Kathy, I'm lost,' I said,

    Though I knew she was sleeping

    I'm empty and aching and I don't know why

    Counting the cars on the New Jersey Turnpike

    They've all gone to look for America.

Marita has been sent off to summer camp on Hudøy Island, and Kari and Johnny each live their own separate lives. He needs a shave. He stomps around, domestic life seems endless, he moves through long evenings spent in demonstrative and morose silences, the flat, the tower block in Bekkelaget. A kind of invisibility has come over them. Johnny, in the office. As if the world frightens him. A terrified little rabbit behind a thin door. Music can be heard through the walls and it pisses Kari off, as she stands in front of the mirror in the bathroom. Over her beauty lie children's bodies that don't resemble bodies. Over her beauty lie also remnants of beauty, it's impossible to stare at such things for too long.

He wears the same clothes almost every day, but Kari has been dressing up. Sometimes she goes out with her new friend, a woman named Liv, who works in the kindergarten in Simensbråten. They go to Garbo. Garbo Pub & Eatery. In summer they go out almost every single weekend and in the autumn, sometimes they go to Garbo on Wednesdays too. Liv likes having an audience. She tells long stories about herself and tosses her hair in a calculated way, she knows the effect all this has on her spectators. She wears high-heeled boots, says she has a *hang-up* about high heels. She wears heavy make-up and teaches Kari how to apply heavy make-up and, afterwards, they light cigarette after cigarette. Liv says the advantage of being single is that she can go home whenever she wants with whomever she wants and then she winks at Kari who is sitting across the table with a beer. And on a regular basis Liv does exactly that. Goes home with whomever she wants. Although mostly it's a kind of rotation, between three or four men who usually sit and drink at Garbo on week nights and at weekends too.

She manages to get up every morning even though she's had a couple of drinks, Liv says and so does Kari.

It's not a problem at all.

The first time Kari meets the guy from Bergen he is at Garbo Pub & Eatery with a whole gang of men, all of them speaking the dialect from western Norway and making toasts and laughing and being so boisterous that Kari wonders whether this will annoy the locals, but nothing happens.

They are from Bergen, the guy from Bergen says afterwards.

Nicest city in the world, he says and laughs and his friends laugh too, because the guy from Bergen is the kind of guy who makes you happy just being around him, she sees that right away, the kind of guy whose laughter is contagious, a man who has that kind of *take on life* (she will later say, to Marita), he makes everything seem simple and uncomplicated and *fun*.

Kari doesn't quite grasp what the guy from Bergen works with. Something or other with containers, he says when they meet again, almost three weeks later, when she and Liv enter Garbo and Kari has put on a little extra make-up in case the guy from Bergen drops in, and he does. When he arrives with his mates, Kari gets up from the bar stool and they hug each other as if they were old friends. He introduces a couple of the new friends, those who weren't there last time. The guy from Bergen looks Kari in the eye and laughs and makes everyone else laugh, but Kari understands that it is only her laughter he cares about. He gets up and comes back with some beers, sets them down on the table and brings over as well a tray of shots of Gammel Dansk.

Hell, he says, we have to have a little one, right? We deserve it. *Ladies?*

That evening the guy from Bergen teaches Kari how to throw darts and he buys beer and they do shots and then they laugh and he stands behind her and shows her how to hold the darts and teaches her to throw *right on*. Liv sits with one of his friends all evening and when it starts to approach closing time, Liv whispers that she— *at any rate*—is ready for an after party.

Kari and the guy from Bergen leave Garbo together, drunk and silly, arm in arm on the way to Liv's flat. He fills her glass and lights her cigarettes. Her laughter feels neither distant nor hollow. The guy from Bergen says she has nice hands. His eyes rest on her thighs. She notices him looking. She feels lighter and lighter. Excuse me, she says, steps slowly over the guy from Bergen, and goes to the bathroom.

It's almost four o'clock in the morning.

I have to get home, Kari says when she comes back into the living room.

The guy from Bergen puts down his glass, stops in the middle of the story he is telling and follows her out into the hallway. There he kisses her carefully on the neck and on her throat, almost imperceptibly unbuttoning the top button of her tight jeans. She hesitates, but only slightly, and then she succumbs and a few minutes later the guy from Bergen pulls his hand up from her crotch and Kari closes her eyes and says breathlessly: Good God, what are we doing?

The guy from Bergen says that he hopes he'll see her again, he really means it. He has work to do in Oslo all the time, he says, down here on Ulvøya Island.

I don't really want to go, Kari says. But I have to.

I don't want you to go either, the guy from Bergen says. He kisses her. She shoves her crotch towards him like a mouth.

I can walk a ways with you, the guy from Bergen says. I just have to get something.

He comes back into the hallway with a half-empty bottle. He throws on his jacket and they leave without saying goodbye to anyone.

She asks about dates, when will you be back, laughs, weaves back and forth on the pavement, the nice shoes, the stumbling and awkwardness and the bottle they drink from, she says when will you be back, loses her way, turns left in her high heels, Bekkelaget and this feeling popping up, the colour violet, the sky, a kind of violet dough that lays itself over her and she has to breath calmly and deeply until the colour disappears and goes away the way fishes go away, breaking up into a swarm of violet lines, like fishes or summer, yeah, like summer, like the kind of violet spots when one looks directly at the sun, like getting lost in those nice shoes and the awkwardness, like laughing and laughing and showing the guy from Bergen whatever, losing the thread of the conversation, climbing over fences and running like kids across grass lawns, through gardens, before Kari pulls down her jeans, snorts and lies down on a bench behind the Nordstrand School, almost naked, *like a child of the sea.*

*

Johnny sits on the couch and waits and imagines the worst, that Kari has been raped, that she's been killed and dismembered and dumped into the Oslo Fjord. He thinks about calling the police. He considers going out to look for her, but where? Garbo is closed. Everything is closed. Where is she? He goes into the bathroom, washes his face and stares at his reflection as he commands: Stop it!

For sure, there's an explanation.

But he cannot imagine what it could be.

When she finally comes home, she says nothing. Can't we do this in the morning? she says, when Johnny asks.

I'm a little drunk.

But Johnny doesn't back down.

It's almost six o'clock in the morning, he says. What the hell.

Go to bed, she says. As if he were a dog.

Just a few hours later Johnny gets up and plods into the bathroom. He doesn't know what to do. He wonders how much he can take, how long he can stand to have this fucking lead weight on his chest. He washes his face. The towel smells of shit. His toothbrush is bushy and foul. The sink is so dirty it's brownish. He goes back into the bedroom, turns on the light and while getting dressed, he asks her one more time, even though she's asleep.

Where the hell have you been? Why did you get home so late? You can't just lie there without saying anything, Kari.

And Kari replies, sort of. Garbo, she says, sleepily.

Until six o'clock? Good God. Do you think I'm stupid or something?

Kari says she's sleeping dammit, but Johnny is relentless and then she rolls over abruptly, like a sullen child, and tells him to lay off, tells him to turn off the light, tells him to get the hell out of the bedroom and leave her alone.

This is not right, Kari. Honestly. What do you expect me to do? Am I supposed to just sit here and wait like some kind of idiot? While my wife is out all night?

Kari sits up with a lurch, as if she has had enough. Throws back the covers and on her way into the bathroom, she says: I was with Liv, OK?

Maybe you should start working again instead, Johnny says. He stands outside the bathroom door.

What the hell does that have to do with anything? I'm on sick leave! she yells. And you know it!

You're clearly not sick at night, he says.

But sarcasm is not Johnny's strong suit. It sounds false and contrived when he tries to be nasty. He sounds like a belligerent child.

He stands in the hallway, hears her peeing.

We just went to Liv's place after they closed, Kari says when she comes out. We sat and smoked and played records.

Just the two of you?

Jesus, Johnny. Aren't I allowed to have a little fun once in a while?

One Saturday morning they sleep together after breakfast, after Marita has taken her bicycle and gone out to
play. He searches for Kari beneath the covers and she
gives in, he imagines her bending over a cat, standing
on a street corner while squinting towards the shop windows of another time, a time when she read woman's
magazines, when she wore a straw hat and sunglasses,
when she watched stumbling little girls at the beach.
She smells of cigarettes, her tongue smells of cigarette
smoke, but Johnny clutches her and embraces her and
won't let go, he searches, finds a gap, in this bed, in this
city, in the dirty kitchen, among the jazz records, Kari
gives in, he doesn't need to ask her to do anything with
her body, because she gets up, lies down, says *like that*,
says *here*, points at him, at herself, at his groin and
hands, she moves as if it were the simplest thing in the
world, then she leans her head back, as if she were coming out of the water, and then she holds Johnny tightly
to her, smiling at him in the leaden bedroom and just
a little further down the road he sees the corner of the
house in Asbury Park, the snowy weather in New York,
a chestnut-brown winter coat, a postcard hung up on a
dirty mirror; when he talks to her, she says: That's how

186

it is for us too, how it will be, don't stop. She says: We'll find each other, we will learn to meet, to choose the neighbourhood and the hour. Don't stop. It's as if she is talking to someone else.

During a dinner party her parents have arranged, Kari drinks too much cognac and insults her mother, who according to Kari doesn't understand anything, who is a stupid social climber of a woman who has not given Kari even one single value in life—that the only thing Synnøve has done is accumulate shit to fill the house with. Everything becomes tense and brittle and stupid. Synnøve is mute and embarrassed and there is nothing worse than an older person who is being humiliated, who is humiliated and ashamed. She gets to her feet, scurries out to the kitchen, clearly upset. Ylva, visibly annoyed with her sister, follows her mother, while Kari looks as if she is sleeping in her chair, her eyes shiny, looking straight ahead of her. Everyone falls silent. Sigurd stares down at the table and Johnny acts like nothing's wrong, tries not to look in Kari's direction. And then she empties her glass and says suddenly that she fucking hates all of them, that she doesn't want to see any of them again, that they can shove all of their money up their assholes for all she cares. She looks like a bird perched on a branch in the fog, waiting.

The following week Johnny speaks to all of them on the telephone. Back and forth between family members. He meets his father-in-law in town and Sigurd takes him to the Grand Hotel restaurant to eat. He cannot accept such behaviour, Sigurd says. She went over the line. Way over the line. Johnny says that he agrees. He doesn't know what's going on with her. He talks to Ylva and tells her that Kari sometimes sleeps so deeply that often during the night he has to roll her over onto her back, and put his ear against her chest to make sure she's breathing. That's when she's been drinking. When she's been out drinking with Liv. I am sleeping horribly, he says and tells them about the dreams; about drowned children and water and waves and coffins, he tells of how stiff and sore his body gets when he sits on the couch in the living room waiting for her, how he can't stand seeing her stumbling around with her eyes transformed, how he can't bear to think about Marita waking up and so he shuts the door in the middle of the night and goes and sits down on a bench in a park.

She is sitting in the kitchen having a cup of coffee. Johnny says she should apologize. He says he doesn't think it's good for them to celebrate Christmas alone.

Kari says he can go to hell. She says it dryly and calmly.

You don't mean that, Johnny says.

You don't know shit about what I mean and don't mean.

She says it in Norwegian.

PART THREE

I grew up, and Mum, Dad and I ate in silence and that was completely normal in our house. They argued and argued but always after I had gone to bed or when I was in my room doing my homework. They thought that I wasn't listening and sometimes I wasn't. Dad said nothing about the guy from Bergen. He watched Mum dress up and make up her face and drag herself to work in the morning, even if she didn't come home until late at night. Dad and I took the tram down to the city centre at weekends, the times Mum didn't want to get out of bed and she smelt, the whole flat smelt, a kind of heavy, foul odour. Mum started moving sort of faster, she didn't complain so much about the music he put on, she talked to me more than she usually did. And that's how it started. That's how Mum started talking to me and afterwards it never stopped, after Dad left and we became *Kari and Marita*, like a door plaque. Do you remember how the autumn was when you were a kid? Do you remember the feeling of sitting inside at home, leafing through comic books you had read a thousand times before, while it rained and the bedspread was nice and warm and the afternoon long and tedious? On days like that sometimes Dad went up to see Marty and I stayed home with her all day. I couldn't make any noise because she was sleeping and when she finally got up, I could do anything I wanted, except open the curtains. She didn't want light. She sat in the kitchen and made coffee on the stove and smoked. I had to leave her alone. Hours passed, and then she sort of came to and started talking. Not to me, not to begin with. She could say things like: Well, about time to air out a bit, maybe. Or: I guess I should get in the shower. Or: Good God, now I've smoked a thousand cigarettes. It wasn't until afterwards that she asked me to come to her. Asked me about school. Where Dad was. Things like that.

We didn't know anything about the guy from Bergen, not until later, after Dad had left and I sat and bawled in the office and listened to Bruce Springsteen. Or maybe he knew. Either way, the guy from Bergen was there. And Liv was there and her daughter, I was forced to play with her when she came to visit and Dad was at Marty's and he hadn't wanted to take me with him. The guy from Bergen was there long before Dad left, I found that out later, here, in Bergen, when Kari sat on the couch and dressed up wearing brand-new stockings. She told me everything. I had to go with her to buy underwear and she'd tell me everything; that she and Dad had barely touched each other for years, that she had tried as best she could to keep things hidden from me, but that Dad was a big-mouth bastard who couldn't leave things be. And I said: It doesn't matter. I said: I don't like it when you call Dad a bastard. I said: I'm glad he told me about Vera and Ann and about George Swensen and about the house. But Mum said that he was just a busybody who didn't know shit.

But Dad said completely different things. He talked to me differently than she did. Or maybe he talked in exactly the same way, but I heard it differently. It's hard to know. Maybe I'm wrong. Maybe I'm romanticizing. More and more often he sat in his office, and sometimes I got the feeling that I almost didn't exist. As if I were a ghost as well, like my sisters and that all three of us walked around in this flat, brushing up against our parents with our death, our bodies cold gusts against everyday life. Sometimes, Dad would come out of the office and call me in. Sometimes, Mum would ask me if I had a boyfriend, if there were any cute boys in my class. Other times, all three of us went into the city centre on Saturdays and I remember liking that; I liked walking between them, taking hold of their hands and hanging there like a bridge. I didn't let go.

The guy from Bergen hadn't been around for months. He had promised he would come, but he hadn't shown up. A kind of breakdown, she said, later. I was visiting Aunt Ylva's house that evening, and Dad called and let us know. Mum is sick, he said. Oh, I said. I could hear it in his voice that he was frightened. I called Grandfather, he said. Oh, I said. We are off to the hospital, he said. Do you want to come? Yes, I said, and then he said he wanted to talk to Aunt Ylva again. We got into Uncle Gunnar's car and drove to Ullevål Hospital, where Mum had been admitted. She had to stay there for a few days, for tests. We were told to go home and Grandfather drove us, because our car was in the shop. It was late and I was supposed to go to school the next day, but Dad said that I didn't have to if I would rather go and visit Mum. We got up and took the tram. She was lying in a different room from the night before, in a bed that I thought was terribly high. She was fine, she said, but her voice was thin and weak, even I could hear it. Dad talked so nicely to her. Said things I can still remember, things I've never heard adults say since. Mum smiled at me while he talked, stroked my hair, said I mustn't worry. Dad kept talking but I was the one she was looking at and I didn't like it. I thought she could have answered him, said something. The next day she was supposed to be released from the hospital and we went there early, but everything was delayed and the doctor was busy and Dad and I sat in the hospital cafeteria and ate beef stew and drank water. I asked Dad if it was serious, what Mum had, and he said no, no, but he didn't really know either and I noticed things like that. Then Grandmother and Grandfather came and we all went into a room where two doctors were sitting behind a desk, who assured us that there was nothing wrong with her. She just needed to rest. One of them said that he had prescribed some muscle relaxants and Dad said: More pills? He sounded like a child when he spoke Norwegian. Grandfather looked at him, as if he wanted to shush him. The doctor looked at Grandfather when he answered: She shouldn't take them too often. But she's so tired all the time, Dad insisted, does she *really* have to take more pills? Aren't there any alternatives? But the doctors had stopped listening to him.

I remember a whole bunch of other things too, fragments, but also things that aren't fragments. I remember my birthday. My 11th birthday. I liked turning 11. It felt like I was on my way. Sort of like, finally out of something. Mum had insisted on inviting the entire class to our house, even though I said I didn't really feel like it. But Kari was still strong at that time. She still talked with a clear voice and she looked me in the eyes and she hadn't turned into all the things she has become now. Most of my classmates actually showed up. I thought that was strange, but the doorbell rang and everyone took off their shoes in the hallway, most had put a tenner in an envelope which they gave to me while they blushed and Mum welcomed them all and Dad stood in the living room and offered soda pop that he poured into these festive plastic glasses with stems he had bought. Then we sat around the coffee table in the living room and had ice cream and hot dogs and drank soda pop and the others looked at Dad so oddly when he spoke English to me. I wanted a trip to the US for my present. That was what I wanted most of all. To go back to see Grandma Dixie and Grandpa Paul. I pestered and pestered. All summer long I said: I will be 11 years old soon and I want aeroplane tickets. I don't remember what I got. Not tickets, that's for sure. But I kept pestering. Dad said that we couldn't afford it. I said that I could save up too. I could save my weekly allowance, I said. One day Dad sat down with me and explained to me how much money was actually involved, if one wanted to buy aeroplane tickets to the US. I thought I'd never be able to save that much money. Not in my whole life. For Christmas that year I wished for a camera. I had seen it in a store on the main street Karl Johan, it was silver coloured and flat and I went on and on about it. On Christmas Eve I sat by the Christmas tree and searched until I found a present that looked as if it could be a camera, and yes, indeed, Grandmother and Grandfather had bought it for me. I was completely over the moon. I could barely fall asleep that night, and lay awake for many hours holding on to my camera,

under the covers, with the light off. After that I started
writing long letters to Grandma Dixie and enclosing
photos of myself, of Mum and Dad and of Oslo. I took
photographs of all kinds of things, of the tram and the
statues in Vigeland Park and of ordinary things. When
the films were used up, Dad took them to the city and
had them developed for me and when I got to see
the pictures, I spread them out on my bed and chose
the nicest ones, which I sent to Grandma Dixie and
Grandpa Paul. Eventually, I saved up for a red photo
album. To start with I pasted in all of the photographs
I took, every single one. But after a while I started
picking out the ones I thought were the nicest, or I
combined photos that had something in common. My
grandfather in particular liked what I was doing. He
often sat down with me and asked me about the photos
and every time he and Grandmother came to visit, he
wanted to see what I had done since the last time. One
day, I don't think it was a birthday or anything—one
day Grandfather came to our house with a Polaroid
camera and a whole carton of film. The first picture I
took with the camera was of myself. I turned the camera
around and pointed it at my face and when it slowly
emerged from the darkness on the paper, I saw myself
in a way I never had before. It was not the same as
how I looked in the mirror and I liked that. When Dad
came to my room and read to me in the evening, I
asked him about it; about mirrors and faces and if

he had many pictures of himself. But he started talking about plane crashes. He said that he dreamt about planes that flew into each other. I didn't understand what he was talking about. A few days later, when Mum had gone out for the evening, he waved me into his office and said that I had to promise never to say anything about this to Mum. Then he showed me photographs of my sisters. We sat in his office and he cried and I had to hold him and I remember thinking *it helps that I'm here*, when he finally stopped shaking. The next day I said I had decided to take a picture of myself every single evening for an entire year. And Dad patted me on the head and gave me a look that almost scared me, before he said again that I must never say anything to Mum about Vera and Ann and the twenty-some photographs.

What could I do?

I promised him anything he wanted.

And then I was sent off to summer camp, on the island Hudøy, and there I fell in love for the first time. With one of the camp counsellors. A dark-eyed boy from the east side. His name was Erik. Erik Cuprud, I remember it well, because he had ears that were a little big and I thought that the last name suited him, since in a way he looked like a cup.

He was 17 and I did everything I could to make him notice me.

Finally he did.

I've already said that, haven't I?

It had been a miserable night, another one. Kari had come home and gone to bed and Johnny had pretended to be asleep. He woke up a few hours later and lay there looking at her. She looked like a wreck. Afterwards she came into the kitchen wearing her bathrobe. Her hair was wispy and messy. She smelt of alcohol mixed in with her perfume and a hundred cigarettes and god knows what else. She barely looked at Johnny, went right to the cupboard and took out a glass that she filled up with water. He kept his mouth shut, kept on making the omelette and called for Marita. He saw that Kari didn't like the shouting, but she said nothing. Maybe they could pretend nothing was wrong. Maybe it would be fine.

He flipped over the omelette, thought about the hole he could feel in his chest on the nights when she didn't come home. He thought that hundreds of thousands of songs were completely right. His heart ached. When he pictured her with other men. When he saw her, all made up and smiling and then he thought about how he was excluded from all of it, pushed out of her life. Not even her happiness had room for him.

He gulped down coffee.

Marita came in and sat down.

When did you get home last night, then? he asked Kari finally, when the silence had become too oppressive, too stupid. As if he didn't know. As if he hadn't lain there and tossed and turned and looked at the clock and finally heard her footsteps in the entryway.

I don't know, she said.

You don't know? he said.

Hey, this isn't improving my mood, that's for sure.

Marita looked up at her parents.

Johnny continued digging into his omelette with his fork.

It didn't take much.

He got off the tram by the Østbanen Railway Station, bought a pair of gloves, a cheap anorak and a hat he thought that Marita would like. He bought rice and canned goods and mincemeat, thought about what Billy would have said if he had seen Johnny going around like a housewife and doing the shopping. When he came home from shopping, Kari went right for his throat. As if she had just been sitting there, waiting for it. He had forgotten to buy something or other that she had explicitly asked him not to forget, that Johnny couldn't even remember Kari having mentioned. She got up off the couch, resigned, self-righteous and sulky, and stated dryly that Johnny hadn't listened, that he didn't seem to care, that what *she* said was clearly not important and that he had to think about the kind of signals that sent. Johnny said he was sorry, he unpacked the groceries, but he also made sure to say that she needn't be so obstinate, at least not to use that tone; he hadn't done it on purpose, if that's what she thought.

Of course I don't think you did it on purpose. Be serious. My point isn't that you 'forget' things, Johnny. But that you don't listen when I talk to you. That what I have to say is so insignificant that you can't even be bothered to pay attention.

God, he said, turned on his heel and walked out of the kitchen.

Later that evening he went over the argument in his head. Kari had locked herself into the bathroom. He thought about what she had said. What he had said. What he could have said. Then she came out into the living room with the make-up heavy and sad on that lovely face. She walked right past him, but he felt the insanity of his love hit him, something stabbing him, like a damn lance buried deep in his chest. And then something abysmal, unfathomable, as he inhaled a whiff of the perfume she wore, which he didn't recognize. It made him gag, almost. That's how love became twisted. Like an old glove. Her beauty, vanished or transformed. The last thing Johnny said before Kari walked out the door was that she looked like a fucking slut, something he regretted the minute he caught sight of Marita, who was standing by the doorway looking up at him.

He prepared a light supper for himself and the girl. Sandwiches, cocoa. He told her that he'd seen two punks on the Youngstorget Square earlier that day. Marita didn't know what a punk was and Johnny explained and mixed sugar water and then they went into the bathroom and wet their hair and gave each other punk hairdos. He asked about school and had her try on the anorak he had bought. She said that she wasn't looking forward to the ski day the following week, not at all.

I can understand that, Johnny said and laughed. I've never been any good at it either. You get that from me. We're just not ski people, you and I.

Not long afterwards Marita started yawning. Johnny cleaned up in the kitchen and went into the living room where he sat down to watch the news. Marita brushed her teeth in the bathroom. He heard the water running from the faucet while he struggled to understand what was being said on the screen.

Are you coming in, she said, afterwards?

Yes, he said. I just want to watch this first, I'll be right in.

Can you read to me, Dad?

Of course I can, kid. Of course I can.

When he came in, she was already under the covers. Turn on the bedside lamp, he said, then I'll turn off the ceiling light. What do you want to hear?

He pulled out a book, but she wanted to hear stories instead: about the time Johnny and Uncle Billy went to California and Johnny dove off of some cliffs which in his faulty memory became higher and higher every time he told her about it. She liked to hear that the Circus Dwarf was called Circus Dwarf because he was so small that his friends often played catch with him like a ball. And when Johnny showed her how they'd done this, Marita put both hands over her mouth and shook with fits of laughter.

Is it true? she said. Is it really true?

Of course it's true, Johnny said. He was teeny-tiny. Teeny-teeny-*teeny-tiny*!

She liked being told about the summer when she and Johnny went to the US and stayed with Grandma Dixie and Grandpa Paul in New Jersey. And even though Marita could remember almost everything herself, she wanted Johnny to tell her about it, because something happened to the summer then, when her father told her about what she'd said and done and where they'd been; she was reminded of the trips they took and Uncle Billy's insistent voice, she saw herself sitting in the car, she could feel the wind blowing against her face when she stuck her head out of the window; she learns the summer of 1975 by heart, Marita, entwines her father's sentences into her own, sees the summer flicker past, slowly and over-exposed; a yellow, shiny summer that ends up by the graves where she and Johnny stand quietly, looking at the names, Vera and Ann and Vera and Ann. From then on her sentences are mixed up, coiling in and out of her father's life, in and out of everybody's life. Marita learns the summer by heart and becomes the girl who sees them pop up on doorsteps, at the bottom of the stairs when she runs down to get her bicycle, when the sisters stand there freezing by the kindergarten or in the middle of Ekebergsletta field where Vera in confusion holds Ann by the hand and refuses to let go.

Johnny stroked her hair and told her stories.

Marita on Grandma's lap an entire afternoon while she looked through photo albums. Marita when she went swimming in the ocean. Marita in New York where she fed the ducks in Central Park, right nearby where Johnny and Kari first met.

Yeah, tell me about you and Mum, she had said. And afterwards the house, the sisters who died, the whole story and their names, *Vera and Ann, Vera and Ann and Marita*, their names all summer, *Vera and Ann* until she comes home and says the names at home and

Kari drops a glass or throws a glass and says Marita must never do that again.

She lay there and could barely keep her eyes open in the blue nightdress that she slept in.

It was nice to have cocoa, she said.

Just don't tell Mum, Johnny said.

No, she said. Where was she going?

To Liv's, he said.

Oh yeah. She stretched, made noises.

You're tired, Johnny said.

Tell me about before, she said, as she turned over onto her side.

Don't you think I should turn off the light, instead? You're tired, Marita.

Please, she said.

And Johnny took a deep breath, dug for stories his daughter could fall asleep to. He came upon a large house close to where Grandma Dixie and Grandpa Paul lived. An abandoned house where we used to play cowboys and Indians in an enormous, overgrown garden, he said. The older boys in the neighbourhood used to throw stones at the rats that zipped between all the boards and all the garbage lying around there.

Ewww, Marita said and her eyelids fluttered. Rats are icky.

And there, in the garden, there was a tree that reached towards the sky, it was like a gigantic hand, Johnny said. Have I told you about Mike?

No.

Mike was a friend of mine when I was little. Once we were there in the garden and we climbed the biggest tree and of course it was all about who could climb the highest. And Mike, he was always braver than all the others. He had a kind of reputation for being the toughest, the most daring. Anyway, on this day Mike had almost reached the top of the tree when, all of a sudden, he slipped and fell and tumbled down to the ground like a sack of potatoes. I can still remember the sound. That was the creepiest of all, the sound of Mike against the ground. A dull and abrupt sound, you almost couldn't hear it. Anyway, he broke both his arms. And you know what happened then?

No, Marita said.

Well, I'll tell you, then. He had to have a cast on both arms and his mother had to wipe his butt for weeks afterwards, Johnny said.

Marita smiled. Ewww! That's gross! she said.

Yup, you bet it was.

And what happened next?

I remember that spring so well, Johnny said. It was in 1950 or '51. The first time Grandpa Paul let me drive the Chevy and I got to sit on his lap and steer while he pointed at the street signs. I can still remember how the hard steering wheel felt against my tiny hands.

How old were you then? Marita asked.

About your age, I bet. A little older. Twelve, thirteen. *Take a good look around*, Grandpa Paul said to me when he let me drive. Take a good look around. You must remember that too, Marita. You have to promise me.

And Marita only just managed to promise him that before her eyes slid shut and she fell asleep.

He went out into the kitchen, made himself a cup of tea and went to sit down in the office. His records, the record player, the four photo albums he'd taken with him when he and Kari moved to Norway. He lit a cigarette. Pulled out a book he'd been trying to read for several weeks. A novel he'd borrowed from Marty. An American novel. *About* America. But it was no good— he read four pages before he discovered with irritation that he'd read the entire passage several times already. He realized it when he read the last sentence.

When you walk it's as if somebody is following in your footsteps.

He had no idea what it was about.

He put out the cigarette and laid his head in his hands. He sat like this for a little while. Maybe five minutes. Ten minutes. Maybe for a full 15 minutes Johnny sat like this, while he thought about the look Kari had given him when she left.

And because there was no way around it he put the blame on the truth.

That was what had hunted them down. Like a bull.

He went out into the living room. Sat and watched television until the sign-off image came on. He switched it off. He changed his sitting position. Lay down on the couch, sat up, pulled out a chair and the night closed in around him until he thought it would strangle him. A few hours passed. He sat up as if in a panic, took a deep breath and looked out towards the empty walkway that seemed to sort of mock him. His heart was hammering hard and stopped hammering quite so hard and Johnny felt stronger, somehow, suddenly, ran his hand over his hair as if in relief, before something surrounded him again. Something dense. The night. Something whispering and snapping. Circles of something. Lots of circles. And he must have dozed off, because the living room became light and dark at the same time, and Johnny sat in the midst of it all, terrified of the circles' horror, the circle of tower blocks around the flat, the circle of walls, the circle of water that surrounded him (that was when he understood that he was dreaming), the circle of algae in the water, the circle of green on the living-room floor, something moss-like and sticky that crept up towards his hands and face. Then, for a moment, everything went white, before the circles appeared again: outer walls, inner walls, steel girders and gratings.

Finally he heard Kari fumbling with her keys out in the hallway.

He heard her close the front door and take off her high-heeled shoes. He saw her reflection in the window. Unsteadily, she reached out an arm and tried to find the wall to support herself against, but she lost her balance and that was when Johnny got to his feet and went out to her.

She had that transformed gaze.

You're going to wake up the girl. For Chrissake, Kari.

He looked her right in the eyes, so she would understand that he was serious. But her eyes were as if pushed into her skull. Dark and empty. There were remnants of white spit on her lips. Her mouth hung a little, as if she had already fallen asleep.

No use in saying anything.

When Kari was like this, she was elsewhere. Nothing reached her. There was a recklessness to it that Johnny could not fathom. He felt sick, but more than anything she scared him. That was the truth.

He helped her throw up and then put her to bed.

He couldn't bear to undress her. Her breath, like someone who's been running or had a scare. How long had they been sleeping on the same sheets? He wiped off her face around her mouth with a kitchen towel, it was the only clean thing he could find.

If something hits you every day, sooner or later you have to hit back, he thought.

Maybe there's nothing much to hit with. But for fuck's sake. I'm burning out.

It's enough.

He woke up on the couch. He woke up Marita and took her down to the city. He could have strangled Kari. Had he been another type of man, he said to himself, he would have beaten the crap out of his wife. When he and Marita came home in the afternoon, Kari was sitting in the living room and watching television with a blanket over her. She hadn't even taken a shower. The thick, smoke-filled air. The smell of hair and armpits and clothes, a filthy life. Marita sat down beside her mother and started telling her about what she and her father had done in the city. Johnny stood watching them for a moment before retreating into his office. He couldn't even stand to hear Kari's voice. It felt as if he'd been deflated, as if something had punched him in the stomach with all of its force. He sat there in the flea-market chair and hung on tight. He heard the voices through the paper-thin walls and thought about the whirlpool-like Sunday tedium, of his daughter's eyes, of all the questions she asked and all the answers he had given her.

He asked himself if it was good enough. If it would do. If he had explained correctly.

He pulled a Charlie Parker live album off the shelf, but before he'd finished listening to the first track, he lifted up the needle and put the record back into the cover. He tried Coltrane. Miles. He tried Charles Mingus, that was what he was looking for.

There he sat, Johnny Richards.

With the door shut.

With Mingus, with Thelonious Monk and Dizzie Gillespie. With Bruce Springsteen's unbearable New Jersey Shore, which is also Johnny's coastline, his board-walks, his streets lit up by the same stars and the same lights that Springsteen sings about.

There he sat, Johnny Richards, while he heard Marita go into her room, the TV being switched off and Kari, the sound of Kari, like a sleepwalker.

Sunday evening in Bekkelaget. Almost night. He puts on his jacket and scarf and leaves the flat. On the stair-way he meets a neighbour who stops to talk about the cold. On the walkway he takes off one of his leather gloves and lights a cigarette. He never managed to get used to the cold, even though winters in New Jersey are as cold as a witch's tit, too. But it was another type of cold here. The day they landed at Fornebu Airport, when he walked down the stairs of the aeroplane and stepped onto Norwegian soil for the first time, the cold hit him in the face with such an ungodly force, it was almost funny. Now he thinks of it as a kind of prophecy. As if the cold had been warning him about this life, and he had been unable to see it. He had had the best intentions, it could be that it blinded him, the hope. He had only wanted for Kari to be all right.

Sunday evening. Night soon.

He turns around at the top of the hill. The wind blows right through him. On the way back he meets another neighbour who is out walking his dog. He stops and smokes another cigarette, while he nods and shivers.

He goes home again. The light in the hallway is turned off. But Kari is still sitting in the living room. He can't bear it. He has to get away. He has to get away from the teacher's lounge and the pupils at school, he has to get away from the tram, from the walks through the park by the royal palace, from long underwear that itches, mittens, gloves, hats. From big stupid shoes that leave deep footprints in the snow.

He goes into his office again. Closes the door.

For 12 years he has walked around, stumbling in this strange language, like a kind of joke that laughs at him.

I'm just a shadow, he thinks, more and more often.

The world hits and hits and I take it. Stand up straight and take it.

She doesn't even notice me any more.

It's enough.

I have to get away.

He pulls out the photo album, and every time he does, he promises himself he'll never open it again, not ever.

But there's no way around it.

The dead girls, still alive in there, in twenty-some photographs that try to cheat death. But nothing cheats death.

He is hungry. Gets up, dries his eyes and waits for the record to finish. Kari is sitting in the kitchen, having a bowl of soup.

You could have asked me if I was hungry, he says.

You could have said that you were, Kari says, and it ends there.

He makes himself a couple of open-faced sand-wiches and goes back to the office. He muses over everything while he chews. Back and forth. Back and forth. Like a stupid kid with a toy he doesn't understand a thing about.

A half hour later Kari pokes her head in and says she is going to bed. It is almost one in the morning. She says she has a headache.

Where is Marita? he says, even though he knows.

She's gone to bed. She's sleeping, Kari says. Her voice is calm. She stands in the doorway with one leg crossed over the other. A kind of mirage. Is it possible? That a person can be turned into one? Maybe he hopes that Kari will come to him. Maybe he hopes that she'll sit down and they'll talk, like before. But neither of them says anything. He is only 42, but he feels old. He is worn out. And scared. Of the kind of death that's been a shameless guest for years, of growing old when he sees his body in the mirror, of his wife's illness when he watches her on the sly.

Neither of them says anything and it's just stupid to keep on standing there looking at each other.

I'll close the door, Kari says.

As she leaves Johnny knocks over a glass with a little milk in it, by accident. He doesn't know why, but he completely falls apart over a stupid little thing like that.

Johnny wasn't sure whether he thought *The River* album was good. It was too long, wouldn't a single LP instead of a double have been enough? He had talked with Marty about it, and Marty thought it was only fitting that Springsteen wrote comedies too. Tragedy's not the only thing worth singing about, you know, he said. Johnny had even permitted himself the luxury of calling Billy, and Billy, too, liked the songs that Johnny didn't like. 'Cadillac Ranch'. 'You Can Look (But You Better Not Touch)'. 'I'm A Rocker'. There were other things on the album, of course, 'Independence Day' for example. 'Point Blank'. The title track, of course. But still. It felt as if Springsteen had betrayed something. Johnny could not quite swallow that carefree kind of joy. He put the record on again and again. The opening was at best tame, limp, deadpan. Neither could he understand what was good about 'Sherry Darling', with that stupid chorus and the braying in the background. He was obsessed with how bad the bad songs on the record were; he called Marty for the seventh time that same week, compared 'Hungry Heart' with 'Jungleland'. You can't do that, Marty said. Can too, Johnny said. He compared 'I Wanna Marry You' with 'Backstreets'. You can't do that, Billy said. Can too, Johnny said. He turned the record over. He listened to all of side two and put on the third. 'I'm a Rocker', for fuck's sake, he said, and Marty or Billy or the ten thousand ghosts Johnny carried around replied: *If you decide to fight the world all by yourself you'll never have peace of mind, buddy.*

Pictures, in the middle of the summer, he and the girl half-sitting and half-lying on the couch, each with their own magazine. She asks and he answers and then she asks about the pictures, can we look at the pictures, Dad? She promises him anything he wants, promises Ann and promises Vera, promises not to say anything to Kari, who has slammed the door shut, already on her way down the stairs, on her way to Liv's.

In one of the pictures, Johnny is wearing a pale-coloured shirt, grey trousers and a V-neck jumper.

You're so young, Marita said.

Yeah, he says. Look how dark my hair was.

Photos that don't mean a thing, a sunny day in 1963, Paul in a red truck outside the factory while Johnny sits on a ferry quay with Tina.

Is that Tina?

That's Tina.

Was Mum jealous?

No. She wasn't.

Oh. Where is this?

Hotel Terminus, Bergen, the summer of 1972, Marita dressed up like a boy. The garden at home in Freehold where Dixie bends over in a flowered dress, cutting plants and flowers while she waves at the camera. Paul in a chequered shirt, on the garden stairs, with Ann on his lap, wearing play spectacles without glass and rompers. The past. He and Kari, the laughter that left you mute, the never-ending smiles against the never-ending photographic ocean. Johnny with the wind in his hair and Kari about to say something; the conversations, their love letters, and now they sit in semi-silence and look out a window towards the darkness that reflects their faces, faces that are the spitting image of the window.

See how pretty Mum was, Johnny says.

Where is that?

Yeah, where can that be?

The silence in the pictures, the frozen smiles, the girls dead and Marita the sole survivor. The pictures make him dizzy. They rob life of its innocence, deprive him of ignorance. He looks at his children and thinks that they were tricked. When the photographs were taken, they were tricked into believing that the world was Asbury Park and the beaches, their grandparents' house and Uncle Howard who brings board games. Not a thing about death, nothing about the little sister who's alive.

On the tram on the way down to the city centre from Uranienborg, he read that Bruce Springsteen was going to play at the Drammen Concert Hall. He had almost reached the Østbanen Railway Station when he saw the little black-and-white advert in the newspaper—a photocopied picture of Springsteen with a guitar and sunglasses, dressed in a white singlet, with a kind of rockabilly hairdo. Johnny pulled the cord, hurried off at the next stop and jogged all the way up to Electric Circus.

They couldn't exactly afford it and he knew there would be hell to pay when he came home, but still.

He wanted two tickets, he said.

The man at the ticket office asked which price class he wanted.

The most expensive, Johnny said and noticed that it was wrong. That the sentence was wrong but he didn't know what was wrong with it.

All right, said the man behind the counter. He bent over, pulled open a drawer and gave him two tickets. It's gonna be great, he said to Johnny, who answered in English. It was simpler.

The tickets cost 128 kroner each, but that afternoon neither Kari nor Johnny had the energy to argue. Marita lit up and talked about nothing else at the dinner table. She also liked the silly songs on *The River*, especially 'Cadillac Ranch'. What's a Trans Am? she asked. Who is James Dean? Junior Johnson? I like it when he sings *Rides just like a little bit of heaven here on earth.*

She asked if she could keep the tickets and Johnny went with her into the room where she attached them to the bulletin board with a drawing pin.

Can we hear the song one more time?

Afterwards she called out into the living room: You ever been to Wisconsin, Mum?

Speak Norwegian, Kari said and went into the bathroom.

Johnny couldn't even be bothered to ask where she was going, just let her go.

But this night would be different. This night she would not come home at all, not until the next day, after Marita had already gone to school.

Johnny can't believe it.

He can't bring himself to say anything when she lets herself in. Her clothes look different. He has already missed one tram. Now he'll miss the next one too. The silence between them like a landslide. This is what life looks like when it's old, when the past and future smell the same, like old trees.

We loved each other. Does that mean anything?

Maybe not.

Maybe it means everything.

But there is no way back.

I love you. I love you. I love you.

But now I am burning out.

Marty takes him in at his home in Bjølsen. He can sleep on the couch, of course he can. Sometimes he wakes up in the middle of the night. Sometimes he can't fall asleep at all and lies there feeling the pain, where it aches when he thinks of Kari and the nights Kari doesn't come home. He gets up, drinks a glass of water, but his mouth tastes of gall, of gastric acid, that green stuff at the very bottom of people. He gets up early and brews coffee. It's his way of saying thank you. He won't get in the way, he says to Marty the first night he sleeps there. He just has nothing more to give. It's all gone. He doesn't know what will happen now.

The day Bruce Springsteen is scheduled to play at the Drammen Concert Hall, 5 May 1981, Johnny goes to a viewing for a room in a flat-share for adults near St Hanshaugen. He has spoken to Sigurd, and his father-in-law has said that he will help out, even though he dislikes that Johnny has moved out. He calls it resignation, and says that *his* generation is not used to giving up as easily as Johnny and Kari are doing. Life is a struggle, says Sigurd and Johnny nods, and the rest of the day he is in an indescribably bad mood.

The room is pretty big, a little cold in the wintertime, says the woman who shows him the flat. Her name is Anne Berit, she is in her mid-30s. She wears round John Lennon glasses that hide big, brown eyes. She shows him the flat and looks at him in a way that he likes. It's been a long time since anybody's looked at him like that. He accepts a cup of coffee. Anne Berit tells him that she has been living here for three months, with someone named Jan Tore, who is a journalist for the newspaper *Aftenposten*, and some Hugo guy, who drank and therefore had to move out.

We don't want to deal with that kind of thing, Anne Berit says.

Of course not, Johnny says.

She tells him about her divorce and when Johnny talks about Kari and Marita, it doesn't feel difficult. It actually feels good to talk to you about it, he says as he drinks the final swallow. Anne Berit becomes a little uncomfortable, but she smiles and he smiles and it's strange, this, but in a nice way, a surprisingly good way. Before he leaves he says that he likes the room, that he is basically ready to move in at any time, if they should decide that they want him there.

Anne Berit says she will have to speak with Jan Tore, but she doesn't expect he'll have any objections. And then she gives him a hug in the doorway and he feels her breasts against his chest and they stand like that for just a tiny bit too long.

OK, he says and laughs.

OK, she says and does the same.

He meets Marita at the National Theatre station and they go and have dinner at a cafe nearby before they meet Marty and Cindy.

Looks like you won't have me hanging around up at your place for much longer, Johnny says.

Great, Marty says turning to Marita. Your Dad here, he's a pain in the ass, kid.

Marita laughs, she asks Marty if he is looking forward to the concert.

You bet I am, he says. And it better be good, at this stiff price!

It's not so bad, he's a cheapskate, you know, Cindy says.

Who paid, you or me? Marty says. Don't listen to her, Marita. She's full of shit, this one. So the viewing panned out?

Yeah, Johnny says and smiles. You can say that. You can say that for sure.

When they reach Drammen they get off the train and follow the stream of boys and girls from the railway station and over to the Drammen Concert Hall. The doors aren't open yet, and they stand around talking to some girls who think it's cool that Marita is with her father, they think it's even cooler that they're all American: Bruce was born in the same place as me, Johnny says proudly, and the girls call out to some boys and soon a whole little gang is crowding around them. Did he know Bruce? No, Johnny says, but he knows people who know him, people who went to school with him and stuff. He himself is a little too old, almost ten years older than Bruce.

Ten years? It doesn't look it, one of the girls says.

Johnny holds Marita by the hand and tells the group that he and Marita were in New Jersey the summer before *Born to Run* came out, but no, he hadn't seen Springsteen in concert. He hadn't even liked him very much at that time, can you imagine?

One of the boys asks Marita if she speaks Norwegian too, and Marita nods and says: *Sure, I was born here*. Another asks what her favourite song by Bruce is and Marita thinks a little bit and answers: 'Lost in The Flood'. Marty pats Marita on the head, looks over at Johnny and both men smile.

What? Marita says. What are you smiling for?

Nothing, Johnny says.

That song's just so cool, kid, Marty says and starts a discussion about whether *Greetings* or *The Wild, The Innocent* is the better record. Three or four from the gang say they haven't heard those albums and Marty snorts, calls them *amateurs* and tells them to shut-up or get lost. You're not entitled to an opinion, he says, and when the boys protest in broken English, Marty says: Hey, don't blame me, blame yourselves, you lazy fuckers.

Dad! Cindy says. Come on! Excuse him, she says to the boys. He doesn't mean any harm.

She's right, Marty says. And I'm right too. Now shut up. What's the better record, then? Come on, tell me. *Convince me.*

Oh God, Johnny says and laughs. Here we go.

A reporter from Norwegian television comes over. Somebody tipped him off, he says, that Johnny and his daughter are from New Jersey.

Yes, Johnny says.

Any chance of getting a few comments? For the music programme *Zikk-Zakk*?

Inside the concert hall the crowd sounds like a huge beast when they shout *Broooce*. Johnny holds Marita by the hand, he can tell that she's a little frightened.

It's gonna be fine, Marita, he says, while they are standing in the queue to buy soft drinks.

Yeah, Marita says. There's a lot of people here, she says. Not so many my age, though.

No, Johnny says. Not everybody has such good taste, you know.

I can't wait, she says. How old were you when you went to a concert for the first time?

I don't know, Johnny says. We didn't have concerts like this when I was young, that's for sure.

What do you mean?

Well, I mostly used to see jazz bands at small restaurants and stuff. This here is something else entirely.

And then the lights went out in the hall and the animal roar again, overwhelming.

Shall we wait with the soda or what? Johnny shouts into Marita's ear.

She looks up at her father and shouts back. Then they go back to Marty and Cindy, through the crowd of people, until they can't get any further and Johnny lifts her up, puts her on his shoulders and the stage lights illuminate the stage.

On with the guitars.

On with the saxophone.

Springsteen who gravely looks out at the black sea of people and gives the count.

One, two, three, four.

And the sound.

That they have in common, Johnny and Marita: Neither of them had imagined that the sound would unleash itself upon them like this. The guitars sort of cut up the darkness in the hall, the voice of Bruce Springsteen summons its strength and takes off, flies out of his mouth, first like butterflies, then like a swarm of razor blades; Johnny with his daughter on his shoulders. Marita who sings along to stories about neon signs and waterfronts, stories about Johnny and Kari, stories that will belong to her for ever. Johnny can feel the sound in his gut. He is filled up with a huge, clear joy, an overwhelming bouquet bound together by grief. When Springsteen begins the number 'Prove It All Night', Marita jumps down from his shoulders and can hardly believe it.

This is fantastic, Dad, she shouts. I love this song!

Johnny looks over towards Marty and Marty nods in confirmation, sure of himself, as if all of this were a present that Johnny and Marita have only just begun to open.

Four days later, after almost two months on Marty's couch in Bjølsen, Johnny received a phone call from Dixie, who with utter calm said: *Your Dad died.* Her voice was cold and distant, and Johnny didn't know whether it was the distance between Oslo and Freehold or if it was other things, other distances that suddenly became clear when people died without warning like this.

Once in a while, when he thought about the girls, when Bekkelaget turned into a murky swamp, he imagined that he knew everything about death.

But he didn't after all, he knew nothing about death.

Your Dad died, Dixie had said.

That was it.

Are you OK? Johnny had asked after a silence that lasted far too long.

I am so angry with him, she answered. I am so terribly angry with him. Then she burst into tears and the telephone line started crackling and Dixie's voice was tossed back and forth in echoes that made him dizzy.

It was as if the world had decided for him. He had to go home and bury a father. After having hung up the phone he sat and stared at a green wall. Then he called Kari, but she didn't answer the phone and he became infuriated with her. It was not a reasonable reaction, but the pain liberated a rage that was also directed at other things—at Oslo and at the miserable person he had become, who couldn't even manage to hang on to his wife. The anger made him feel strangely invulnerable, but that wouldn't last. Afterwards other things would come. He had to do his duty, as a man. As a son. The last time he had buried his children. It was wrong to bury children. One should never be obliged to bury children. Now he was going home to perform a kind of ritual. And it felt, if not good, at least, right.

He called Sigurd. His father-in-law would of course lend him money; he then put himself on a flight to New York, fastened his seatbelt and waved at the stewardess. He wanted gin, but mostly he wanted to sleep. Half the night he stood at the back of the plane and smoked cigarette after cigarette and wondered why the sleeping pills weren't working.

And Kari became *Kari and Marita*, like a door plaque.

Johnny has told his mother that he wouldn't be arriving for a few days and that she need not pick him up at the airport, he has already made arrangements. He knows that it's selfish. He knows he should have made a beeline straight out to her, but he couldn't bear having to hug that tiny body, having to lay his head on her shoulder and inhale her, having to look at her skin and the feeling of her smooth and stubby fingers stroking him. Her, all of her, across his hand, across his cheek, over his hair.

First he had to come home alone.

He had planned on taking a bus to Billy's, but when he comes out into the arrival hall, Billy is there already, with his little girl on his arm. He hugs Johnny so hard you'd reckon it was Billy who had been away all these years and not him.

You look good, Billy says. You're exactly the same.

But a lot of time has passed.

Several years.

Loads of days and nights have passed and you can't look the same as before, you can't be the same.

This, Billy says, is the famous Miss Jenny Jones. The little girl smiles and reaches out a tiny white hand and greets Johnny. Billy puts her down and heaves Johnny's suitcase onto a trolley, then they walk out into the sunshine, out to Billy's car in the car park. Billy is eager and talkative, he barely watches the road while he's driving. At first when they get out on the highway, the cars are whizzing past them like the devil, and Johnny makes jokes, says that Billy drives like an old woman. Jenny laughs in the back seat and Billy says the she mustn't listen to Uncle Johnny, because he is full of baloney.

Oh, he's a poet, Johnny says, and doesn't even know it.

Interstate 95, the New Jersey Turnpike. Past Elisabethport and Bayway. Over the bridge, towards South Amboy and Old Bridge. Just ruins on this side now, Billy says. Empty apartments and sniffing kids and the remains of god knows what. These are strange times, buddy.

When they approach Freehold, they talk about which stores still exist and what's there now where before there was nothing. The shopping centre is new, Billy says. Johnny looks at the glass-covered building. Hell, he says. It's huge.

Yeah, Billy says, a little proud. You want to see it?

They stop, go in and each have a hamburger at McDonalds. Jenny is beside herself with joy.

It hits him. The heat and the noise, so unlike Norway, all the tattered teenagers hanging out on street corners as Billy drives in towards Fairview. Pizza shops a Norwegian would never in the world have dared to enter. People like that can cut you up with a look, Johnny says without thinking and Billy looks at him and smiles uncertainly. Johnny tries to say something about Norway and his friend nods mechanically and drives in and out of streets, to the left, to the right, both hands on the wheel, trying to look the same as before, leaning back and nonchalant; a 40-year-old who still sees an 18-year-old kid with taut skin in the rear-view mirror, slender limbs that have long since disappeared into too many junk-food meals.

When Johnny talks about Norway, Billy doesn't really listen. He can't grasp the silence Johnny starts talking about; the afternoons with the state television channel on, the frozen grins on everyone he met, the cold Oslo winters and the snow that blanketed the cars and muted all the sounds, as if the entire city was a fucking sound-proof interrogation room, a damn pressure chamber.

Here in New Jersey everything is different but, then again, it's not.

1981: Your Dad died.

Billy turns into a side street, drives into an entryway where an older man wearing overalls waves the car in with an absent but friendly expression.

We have to pay to park the car here at night. We found out that we had to, even though it costs a little money, Billy says. If you park out on the street, you'll fucking find nothing there the next day.

That's how things have become.

Johnny takes the suitcase in his hand and follows Billy and his daughter. The paint on the stone building they live in is peeling, and outside there are three young boys who say hello and ask who Johnny is.

This here, Billy says and puts his arm around Johnny—this is my best and oldest friend. He has just come back from a long journey.

Oh, one of the boys says. From where?

Guess, Johnny says.

Canada, the boy says.

No, Johnny says.

Baltimore, the other one says. My father has been to Baltimore.

No, Johnny says. Not Baltimore. Shall I give you a hint?

Yes, they say in unison.

It's outside the US.

Outside?

Yes, some other place. Not in America.

Mexico! the third one shouted.

No, Johnny says.

I know, Jenny says suddenly. She is standing and holding Billy's hand and half hiding behind him.

Yeah? Johnny says and looks down at the little girl. Let's hear it, Jenny. Where have I been?

Norway, she says, shyly.

Yes! Johnny says. Norway. That's right.

What? the boys say. Where's that?

Johnny puts down his suitcase in the little room that Billy has prepared for him. Then he goes out into the living room and says hello to Sarah, Billy's wife, who smiles bashfully and extends a limp, white hand. After having exchanged a few compulsory pleasantries, she excuses herself and goes into the kitchen with their daughter.

She's great once you get to know her, his friend says and Johnny nods and says absolutely, absolutely, she seems great.

Good to have you home, Billy says, when they've sat down.

It's good to be home too, Johnny says. But he just says it. He doesn't know if it's good to be home. He doesn't even know if this is his home any longer, if the house he is returning to has anything to do with him at all.

It's a shame about your father, Billy says. My condolences, I . . . I didn't want to say anything while Jenny was listening . . . she would have asked and then . . .

Yeah, I know, Johnny says. Thanks, Billy. I don't know if I've understood it yet. I don't know. Maybe when I get home. I don't know.

Sarah comes in with Coca Cola and glasses and sandwiches. Then she disappears into the kitchen again.

It was just a matter of time, Johnny says. He was already working himself to death 30 years ago. It wasn't exactly like he hadn't been told.

He was always so rough, Paul, Billy says. Do you remember the time we stole tools down at Clinton's and your father came and picked us up when we got caught? I thought I was going to wet myself.

Yeah, Johnny says. But he doesn't know what he's saying yes to. He drinks up his Coke. Sarah comes in and says that she and Jenny are going out. Johnny says that the sandwiches were fabulous.

After his wife has gone, Billy gets to his feet, goes over to the stereo and asks Johnny if there is anything special he'd like to hear.

No, Johnny says. Just put on whatever you want.

He starts flipping through his records and Johnny takes in the silence. Notices how heavy his head feels. The sounds from the street. He hasn't heard these kinds of sounds for more than six years.

I often thought about coming over, he says. But it never came to anything. It's expensive travelling from the end of the world, he says, but catches himself and laughs, so that it doesn't sound so serious.

It's the world's fucking asshole, Norway.

The world's asshole? Billy says. I thought that was here. This hole here can't be anything but the asshole of the world, if you ask me.

How does one talk about one's dead father? On the aeroplane he had drained glass after glass of gin, looked out into the darkness and thought about a thousand things that had to do with everything and nothing. Memories, fragments of conversations, a glimpse of his father in blue overalls, in a suit when he went to the factory in the morning, the rough hands that he folded so childishly when he said grace before dinner. It was perhaps nobody's fault, the mess with his father. So many things had played a part, Howard's suicide and the money and the girls' death and the trip to Norway. Johnny didn't like to think about it but they had yelled and yelled and afterwards it was not possible to take the yelling back. The sound of it continued into the future.

Water under the bridge, Paul had said, but the girls were dead then and all such phrases sounded monstrous.

How long you staying? Billy asked.

I don't know, Johnny said. I haven't thought that far ahead yet. I'll see when I get home. Could be that Mom needs me here for a while. I don't know.

Kari, then? And Marita. Couldn't they come?

Marita has school. And I moved out a few months ago. I was going to write to you and tell you, but there have been so many things. Sorry.

Really? No way, *Jesus*, that's nothing to be sorry about, Johnny. What happened?

Yeah, what happened? Johnny says and smiles. I ask myself that too, all the time. What the hell happened, right? If only one knew, Billy. If only one knew that.

But you're OK? I mean apart from this with your father, of course.

It's all right. It was better not living with her any more. At least I sleep better at night, let me put it that way.

OK, Billy says. I don't really understand what you mean, but you go ahead and talk about it if you want.

Maybe some other time, Billy. It's all a bit much right now.

I get it, he says. It's up to you.

Are you going to put on a record or what?

Billy puts on a Simon & Garfunkel record and asks if Johnny has heard that they'll be playing a free reunion concert in Central Park, in the autumn.

No, I didn't know, Johnny says.

That'll be good, Billy says. It'll be great.

Sure it will, Johnny says. It'll be great.

The sun shines in through the window. Johnny gets up and looks out. A newspaper blows across the grass on the other side of the street.

And you? Johnny says. How are things with Sarah? How old is Jenny now? They look out into space, they empty the bottle of Coca Cola. Billy tells him about Sarah and Jenny. Everyday things. Curiosities. Things they say and do. Johnny nods and falls silent, asks about old friends. They speak in starts and stops, but sometimes it loosens up. It's good to see each other again, they both know that. After a couple of hours Billy looks at his watch, gets to his feet and says: OK. Come on, there's something I have to show you.

The place is full of old friends who have been waiting for his homecoming. Johnny Boy Richards from a former New Jersey, a place in the past; Johnny Richards from those endless nights that only exist wrapped up in hardened memories, something cement-like but something they all share, after all.

He is surprised and overwhelmed and touched and his friends hug him and slap him on the back and say that they are sorry about his father, it was so damn unexpected, how are you doing, really? Did you just arrive? You had no idea about this, did you? Fuck, man. It's good to have you home again.

Johnny from Freehold. He who once upon a time was supposed to become something big. But then he also came home, the way all the others came home. Even though it wasn't from the war. But who knows. Maybe the war got in the way of Johnny's greatness too. His life. *His* war. A war other than the big one, but a war nonetheless.

They've been waiting for him, Dick Merrit, Sol, who has gone bald and is as thin as a pencil. Eric and Tipp, Bobby Wilenz and Luke, The Doc. They have made a banner that they've hung up above the bar, *Welcome home, old sport.* Welcome home to the valley of death it could just as well have said.

*

All the old friends. The old life. As if the past had been taken out of a box for this evening only, unfolded like a sheet full of holes that could still be used. For once they were all together. That's what Tipp said, a little later in the evening, after drinking beer and shots with both hands.

Your dad had to go and fucking die to get these bastards here, Tipp said.

Doc tried to stop him. Tipp, he said. Come on man, show a little respect, will you? You're not so wasted that you can't behave, right?

It's fine, Luke, Johnny said. Let him carry on.

See? *You dick*. The only thing they give a damn about is their kids, Tipp continued, addressing Johnny. Never any fun any more. Shit man, your dad had to go and fucking die to get you to come home so these assholes would come crawling out of their houses.

Well, Johnny said. I'm really glad you all did, though. He just managed to hold back the tears.

Hell, Tipp said. Gimme a hug, man. He hugged Johnny. You too, you asshole, he said to Doc. Come on you pussy.

Even Tina Scott was there and that was completely unexpected, but still it felt more right than anything else. She had grown thinner, was drawn, saggy. Her hair was long and straight and dull. Her skin, which had once been brown and smooth, was now blotchy and coarse.

Hi Johnny, she said. And mournfully, listlessly she lifted her beer glass in his direction.

She sat down beside him. He hugged her against him. He put a hand on her thigh, on top of her hand, threw his arm over her shoulder, kissed her on the cheek and the conversations got more and more sniffly, more and more sentimental as the hours passed. It was like a light. He had the urge to burst into tears, let his arms hang straight down and starting honking like a child.

Doc was the first one who said he had to go home.

It was almost half past one and he had to get up early to go to work the next day, he said. Johnny sat in a corner with Tina and Tipp and Billy, who was red-eyed and quiet for a long time before he trotted out to the toilet to throw up. Tipp was a sissy, Billy said, before throwing back yet another tequila. The alcohol sort of lifted things away, veils or those kind of huge stones that are used to close up caves in fairy tales. Everybody asked everybody else about things that were mostly hidden, that did not want to be found. Billy almost fell asleep in his chair. Then he went and threw up again and everything spun like a carousel, Johnny's world too. But he liked the intensity. His father stood on the outskirts of it all. To Johnny he seemed to be dressed in some kind of armour. On the outskirts, all of his friends and Tina Scott, whose arms moved towards him like swirls of smoke.

Are you going to sleep over at my place? Billy asked finally.

Johnny looked at the clock and looked at Tina and she said: I don't mind staying.

Good night, you asshole, Tipp yelled when Billy went home to his family, to his child, to all those who were living and not dead.

Afterwards, Tina and Johnny and Tipp went out into the night. Tina and Johnny stood on a street corner hugging Tipp for half an hour before they could get away. Then they walked slowly, arm in arm, towards the apartment Tina rented, which she earlier that day had meticulously picked up and cleaned.

He goes home the next day. His mother picks him up at the bus station. He sees her before he gets off, lifts his hand and greets her through the window, breathes, lifts his suitcase. She looks good, he says and Dixie answers by asking if Johnny can drive, she's not used to driving any more, she doesn't have the strength for it.

But I could have picked you up, Dixie says.

It was just as easy taking the bus, he says.

Yes, she says.

Mom is a tiny lady who is getting tinier, Johnny thinks, when they park and she gets out of the car. He puts his things in his old room. Dixie goes down the stairs to prepare a little something to eat, she says, and Johnny sits on the bed and looks at some pennants, postcards, a picture of Ann and Vera and one of Marita, who in this life share the frame, who in the life of photographs stand side by side, their bodies resemble one another's, their eyes, hands, and then he has to look away and it doesn't help to look away and then he leaves the room and closes the door. Dixie has set the table. The window she looks out of is grey and her face is grey and Johnny thinks that even his soul is grey on days like this. But the house is immaculate, as it always was in his childhood. He doesn't understand it. He has never understood how his mother could be bothered to keep it like this. Day in and day out. It looks exactly the same as it did when he left. The same smell, even, everything as if suspended, as if nothing could escape anything.

They eat and ask each other questions carefully. About Kari and Paul, about the trip, about his death. His mother's face twists, but she holds back the tears. She is angry with Paul. So terribly angry with Paul. She forces Johnny to eat one more pancake, even though he says he feels a little sick. She goes through the conversations she has had with the funeral parlour, word for word, correcting herself every time she believes that she has presented an incorrect detail, no matter how small and insignificant it is.

In the afternoon they drive down to Higgins Memorial Home on Center Street, where Johnny and his mother and a dozen others attend the simple service.

He holds Dixie's hand. He hears sobs from the rows of benches behind them, but he does not cry. It's all dry, everything inside him seems to crackle, as if it could catch fire at any moment. His father lies there with his eyes closed and Johnny doesn't want to look at him, but he knows he has to. His father's white powdered face lights up the room like a moon and all Johnny can think about is how are he and his mother going to be able to talk about him. Johnny feels almost nothing at all, he doesn't know what it is, this which is not anything.

People whom he hasn't seen in more than 20 years hug him with their skinny, old bodies. They put their arms around Dixie and blow their noses into handkerchiefs which they put back into their pockets. It is a heartbreaking scene; he feels as if he is looking in through a window, as if his father's death is some kind of grotesque exhibition. He can hardly wait for it all to be over. Till he can close the bedroom door and sleep and sleep and sleep.

I'm glad you came home, says Nathan Forster, one of Paul's oldest friends. He has no teeth left and Johnny holds his breath when Nathan stretches out his arms to hug him.

He was a good man, your father, Nathan says. Stubborn as a mule! But a real man. A true American.

Back at the house, Dixie has ordered finger sandwiches, and two young women—neighbours whom Johnny doesn't know—have set the tables with white table-cloths and lit the candles and put out the food. Johnny ends up seated next to Hayley Rubens, one of Paul's secretaries from the 1960s, who after having spoken about his father as if he had been some kind of saint, talks at length about her own medical history, about the medications she must take and the hospital stays that have become more and more frequent and more and more expensive.

When the house is empty, it is an indescribable relief.

I have to go lie down for a bit, Johnny says. Or do you need some help?

No, no, his mother says. Go ahead and rest. Jessica said she would help me. She will be on her way soon, I'm sure.

Johnny has slept for several hours, a sound and deep and dreamless sleep. Dixie sits and watches TV and when he comes down, she says thank you and holds his hand for a long time between her own two hands. Afterwards, she opens a bottle and pours Johnny a drink. He died in the car, she says and Johnny knows all this, but he has to hear it again. That's how death is. A kind of circuit loop. He parked and then he died,

Dixie says. Typical. He just managed to get home. He couldn't do things halfway. They said that his heart was grey and as hard as a stone. The doctor had been telling him the same thing for more than ten years. Don't overexert yourself. Stop eating so much greasy food. Get a little exercise. Don't drink heavy liquor. Dixie pours another drink and Johnny looks at her and they sit there and drink until they can scarcely recognize each other. He cries, at first quietly, but then it's as if something bursts and he cries for everything, for everyone, for Vera and for Ann and for Kari who doesn't come home and for his father who he isn't grieving for and hell if he didn't die with a stone in his chest. And he cries for Marita who is alive and for Tina's sad face and for his mother who looks like a stupid little doll, a kind of bird with dead eyes.

The next day he wakes up with his clothes on. He is cold. He has been freezing for hours, he thinks as he suddenly feels the headache hit him like an axe across his forehead. He gets out of bed and goes into the little bathroom in the hallway. He hears the radio from the floor below. His mother has already made breakfast, he goes down the stairs and sits down to eat. Then he opens her medicine cabinet and he goes out into the garage, where he sits on a stool and starts going through his father's things. Bags of postcards and *Playboy* magazines. Ring-binders containing bookkeeping documents and cardboard boxes full of broken tools. He finds an old overcoat and puts it on, tilts up the garage door and feels the sun stab him in the eyes. The headache has begun to release its grip. He stands on the lawn in front of the house. His mother waves at him absently from the kitchen window, and he waves back and starts to walk away, with his hands in his pockets, where he finds an open packet of chewing gum and a pack of cigarettes with three broken cigarettes in it. He walks and walks in the heat. After a few blocks he stops and buys a creamy ice-cream cone, which he eats as he trudges on, through Freehold, with both feet solidly planted in Freehold, finally home, in America.

He stops on a street corner, hails a cab and asks the driver to take him out to Asbury Park.

That's gonna cost you, the driver says. There are buses that go down there, you know.

Just drive, Johnny says. I have the money.

The streets. A thousand and one nights, in America. Your father died and the plane trip across the Atlantic, a black, black hole in the world. A black night with his clothes on and his mother's small eyes. Life and Tina Scott who wakes him up, but he is already awake.

Are you crying? Tina had asked. And the streets. And his mother. And the wind, the open car window while he's being driven out towards Asbury Park.

Everything that's burning.

Of course I'm crying, he'd said. Damn straight I am.

He pays and gets out. The waterfront bar where he used to sit and drink beer is gone. So are the girls who glided back and forth on their roller skates on the boardwalk. But the fortune tellers are still here, and a few of them are sitting outside in the summer wind, in the salty sea scent that cools him off, Johnny Boy, standing at the intersection between his old life and this. He walks. He looks up at the rusty Ferris wheels, could be at phantoms, ghosts playing hopscotch on the pavement. He recognizes the crack in a wall by a butcher's that is locked up with bars and chains. He sits down on a stone by the pier. He sees glimpses of his youth, of high-school life, of little girl angels and cars with flames painted on the bonnets.

He just sits there, Johnny Richards, for the time being, on the boardwalk in New Jersey, where he looks out at the same waves and the same seagulls of 20 years ago, while everything sort of closes in around him like an overcoat even larger than the one he is wearing.

His dead father's coat.

And then he runs his hand over his hair and thinks what the hell am I doing here.

A month later he goes to LA, to look for the end of the world.

(*Silence*)

In all of Johnny's dreams—glass by glass, over there at Terry and Mona's house.

Another life, but the same life.

A dream Marita starts dreaming too.

A dream she inherits—the sound of rubber tyres and everything that comes afterwards.

The future.

The future that is so bright or yellowed or like a wellspring, Johnny says to her after he moves out, after he explains a number of things to her and moves in with a friend in Bjølsen, for now.

The future is an ugly, ugly secret, kid.

That's because this is how we talk to each other, Dad. You and I. This is how we talk in this story. *I love you.*

I love you too, kid.

Are you going to leave us?

Grandma Dixie is alone now. I have to go home.

I'm alone now too. Everyone is alone. Mum suddenly wants me to call her Kari when we meet people she knows, people I don't know. They are wearing perfume, you can smell it from way off.

Your Mum and I don't really know how to talk to each other any more. All we do is remember things we don't want to remember and don't want to forget. Time paints pictures, that's what time does.

What kind of pictures?

People eating people up. Animals eating animals up. Life eating up life.

I like you calling me kid.

I know. You are my little kid, my only little kid.

Are you leaving us now? When are you coming back?

Oh, I'll be back.

Promise?

(*Silence*)

Grandpa Paul is dead, you know. My dad. He is my dad. Was. You liked him a lot. And Grandma Dixie. I wish we could live in America. I wish I didn't have to have this feeling of always being short of breath. It's too bad we have no money. Too bad everything went to hell, kid. It started and then it continued and that's life. It never stops. Or maybe one day it stops, but then it's over, or maybe that's when it begins, nobody knows. Only God knows. If he even knows anything at all. Maybe God is sitting on the edge of a bed too, and his heart has long since burst and shrivelled and this here . . . (*points at his chest*)

Is it grey?

It's grey all right. I never learnt how to live here.

Are you leaving now?

Yes, now I'm leaving.

Where you going?

Home.

Are you coming back?

Oh, I'll come back.

But you're not promising.

Sleep comes in jerks, and then it's there as if it has come to stay for ever. Marita dreams about seahorses and crabs and about Grandma Dixie's face in a picture Johnny has in his wallet, about the house where her sisters died, where also Marita was born even though she was born in Norway.

Tell me, she says.

OK. Come in, sit down here.

What's the name of this record, Dad?

Bird, it's called. Him. See. We used to go and listen to bop in the place above the bowling alley on Beacon Street. Your mother also came along a few times, but she put her hands over her ears.

Before or after the accident?

Before. Before. After the accident they stopped playing bop and Radio Record Shack closed and we couldn't dig down into the 19-cent box and listen to records in a cubicle before we decided to buy them. Are you hungry?

No. Are you?

No. I'm thirsty. How are you doing, kid?

I dream about them.

(*Silence*)

I dream that we are girlfriends.

(*Silence*)

Everyone dreams, kid. It's not dangerous. I promise.

*

(*Silence*)

Dad?

Yes?

Have you already left?

I've left.

But you're coming back?

I'm coming back. I am.

Sometimes I run like I'm possessed. My body itches. I have no peace, but the pounding in my chest helps. I usually run across Ekebergsletta field. Nobody is faster than me. You should have seen me. Birds follow me. They fly right above my head and I understand them. Sometimes I talk to them. Isn't that strange?

Nothing is strange, kid. Nothing is curious or out of the ordinary in this story. Birds listen.

Sometimes I think that I am going to take off like they take off. Have you left already?

I've left. One morning I was gone, and I don't know and neither does your mother when all of the bad stuff started. We used to love each other, you know. There are 15 double-bolt locks on all of the doors of this story, kid.

(*Silence*)

Afterwards, Mum and I became *Kari and Marita*. Like a door plaque.

I was sorry I had to leave, you know that, right?

I know, Dad. You were so thin.

I was so thin and then I had to leave.

And afterwards it was so empty. I don't like thinking about the flat. Almost never.

I can't think about it either.

Mum wanted me to call her Kari. She came home late and smelt of beer and cigarettes. Mum was suddenly called Kari and not Mum and Mum said she loved her little child. I'll never let you go, sugarplum, she said, but she had already let go of so many things.

I didn't want to leave, but I was so thin. Do you remember?

I remember. There are many things that I remember. I took pictures and Granddad picked me up in his car sometimes and I stayed with them for several days, then Mum came and got me and then there was always hell to pay. I'll never let you go, Kari said. That's what she said when the guy from Bergen didn't show up and she started bringing other men home and the next day she was always so unhappy, so awfully, awfully down in the dumps. Then she said: I can't lose you, little dearest. Then she said: I can't lose you, because if I lose you I'll die like all the others in this fucking story. I'll lose you to that fucking garden and to that other life by the fucking tree and then I'll lose you to the girls and the yellow dresses and to Seaside Heights and to death. She said that.

(*Silence*)

Have you left now, Dad?

I've left. I left many years ago. And then, when I finally came back, I kept going, here, to LA, to look for the end of the world. That's what I said to Tina and she said: If you want, I'll go with you. But I couldn't ask her to do that.

I have always comforted you.

You have. It may not be right, but it's true.

When you left I sat in your chair and listened to Bruce Springsteen and cried for months. Mum was suddenly called Kari and came home in the middle of the night, sometimes she came home at dawn and I was awakened by her steps in the hallway. The full moon that lit up my room just a couple of hours before was almost gone, had become one with the sky and our building and everything else. I heard the voices. Kari brought people home with her and they made noise in the living room and they danced and, afterwards, they went out into the hallway and made even more noise, and sometimes Kari played some of the records you left behind, those you listened to when you were mellow and thinking about America and then everything grew quiet and then they got noisy again.

I called you, right?

Yes. You called. And you wrote. But Mum thought you didn't call me enough. That you didn't write enough letters. She hated you after you left. And Granddad did too. He tried to restrain himself, but he said all kinds of ugly things about you.

I understand that, kid. Kari is his child. I am just some guy who waltzed into her life with something

I believed to be happiness in my hands. But then it turned out to be something else. Know what I think?

No.

That happiness is like water in your palms.

Like water?

Yes, like water. Like when you turn on the faucet and make a kind of cup with your hands and fill your hands with water. That's what happiness is. Like the water. It's a matter of not spilling it. But there's no way. It's inevitable.

(*Silence*)

How's California?

I don't know. Maybe I'm happy here.

Are you?

Maybe.

(*Silence*)

Did she really play my records after I left?

Yes. But only at night. I was almost never allowed to put them on, she got angry and sulky every time, but one day I went completely nuts and then she understood, I suppose, and said nothing more about it. I bit people, you know.

I know. Maybe that was my fault.

No. It was my fault. I was the one doing the biting.

Did you go crazy?

Yes. I went crazy. I missed you so much. And I missed Mum, and then I went crazy one day when Liv and her daughter were visiting and I attacked Liv's daughter and Liv took hold of me and then I bit her and Kari dragged me away and held me back and afterwards she cried and called me little doll, little pumpkin, golden girl, things like that. Kari sat in her bathrobe, made up like a clown. And she cried and I felt sorry for her, but I couldn't stand Liv or her daughter. Mum, I said, don't cry Mummy, please. And she said she'd been unbelievably beautiful, that the boys used to chase after her, in America, before the accident. Is that true?

That's true. She was strikingly beautiful, your mother.

She said people thought she looked like a famous actress. I said she just had to stop crying. Kari, you look a lot like that actress, she said. That was what they said to me, she said. But I just didn't want her to start crying again.

She was very, very beautiful, your mother.

Once in a while when she was unhappy at night, she woke me up. When the men had left. Then she spoke English to me. Her mouth smelt. And then she would take out photographs. Sometimes it was pictures of Marilyn Monroe, other times of Audrey Hepburn and once she said she was going to show me pictures of Ann and Vera. She just had to find them, she said.

I couldn't leave them behind in Norway.

I knew that, Dad. I knew she wouldn't find the album and I knew that I mustn't say that I'd already seen the pictures—it's our secret.

It's our secret.

But she looked for them. Sometimes, she would get it into her head and she would turn the whole place upside down. But she didn't find them. Once in a while, she sat down and tried to explain to me what they looked like. Sometimes she said: You look most like Ann. Other times: You look exactly like Vera.

(*Silence*)

Then what happened, Marita?

Then what happened. That used to be my question.

It's true. And do you remember what I used to answer when it was late and you had to go to sleep?

Yes. You answered: And the weather changed, summer came and so on.

Yes.

It happened to us too. The weather changed, summer came and so on. But before that I bit one of the girls in my class because I was angry and the girl pissed me off with that stupid doll-voice of hers. And a few days later there was a boy who was talking shit about my trousers and I just about strangled him before they finally managed to pull me away from his throat. He was bluish for all of fourth period. He shook and hiccoughed, the wimp. The child shrink they sent me to asked about you and about Kari and about the accident and I said that the girl had a doll-voice and that the boy had deserved a good smack, because he was so damn cheeky and somebody had to teach him a lesson. And the shrink asked me about you and Kari and about the accident and I told her about the head that was almost torn off, that I looked like both of my sisters, we're almost identical, doctor, I said and afterwards I asked her if she was a real doctor or was she just another idiot?

And Kari?

Kari and the guy from Bergen. And the other men.

(*Silence*)

It's strange, that it's you who is telling me about such things, kid.

I have to tell you about it: the guy from Bergen was for the most part happy and talkative, but every now and then Kari said that he just wanted to be by himself, and then he went back to Bergen and Kari started talking to herself and then I had to go with her to the doctor to ask for pills and one day the doctor said no and Mum made a scene in the doctor's office and from then on she went to another doctor, one who didn't ask so many damn questions, she said. But the guy from Bergen always turned up again and I heard him say sorry, my dove, sorry, sorry, sorry; look, I brought you flowers and chocolate and a little something in my breast pocket. And they cried and suffered and love was full of booze and snot.

(*Silence*)

Then what happened?

Kari made up her face like a doll. The sun lit up the fjord the days that Kari had a visit from the guy from Bergen. One day she said she was going to Bergen on holiday with him, and I had to stay at Aunt Ylva's house for a while. Aunt Ylva was fine, but she talked as if I was mentally retarded and I didn't like that. When Kari came home from Bergen, she had a new hairdo and new shoes and her mouth was as red as a rusty rose. The guy from Bergen said that pretty soon they could move in together, she told me, and for a few weeks the guy from Bergen lived with us and then he left again. But Kari didn't cry. She whistled and smiled and picked up and cleaned the house. One day she asked me to start packing my things and she talked about the guy from Bergen all the time and she said to me: I love you golden girl, the future is coming now, my love.

(*Silence*)

And then we moved to Bergen and I had to grow up. That's how it was.

(*Silence*)

Have you already left, Dad?

Yes. I was the one who left. One day I woke up, opened the closet door and threw trousers and shirts into a bag before I went in to see you and tried to explain things that almost couldn't be explained to a child. Afterwards I was gone, but I was still close by. I called you, right?

Yes, you called.

And I met you at the National Theatre station, at the square Youngstorget, outside the department store Glasmagasinet. Do you remember? And then we went to Kaffistova together and I had coffee and you could order whatever you wanted.

Yes.

Do you remember Marty?

Yes. And Cindy too. I thought she was pretty.

Marty helped me, you know.

Yes. He helped you.

It wasn't easy, kid. You grew and grew. One day you wanted braids, latchkey kid. And then you wanted to have short hair like the boys and I cut your hair, but the bangs turned out all crooked and we laughed about it, but when Kari came home she got angry and said that you couldn't go to school looking like that. What would they think, the teachers. What kind of parents would they think we were.

(*Silence*)

You asked and asked. And then what happened? you asked. And I answered.

Yes, you always answered.

And then you had to grow up?

Yes. The future started in Bergen. It was raining when Kari and I arrived on the train. I was wearing a blue coat that was too hot. Afterwards, on the same day, the rain let up and then the guy from Bergen had already shown us the little house where we would live, at least for a while. A cosy little house, in an alleyway out in Nordnes. It smelt of dust there and the floor was crooked but it was cosy. Kari thought it was very cosy. The first night I lay awake. I heard the rain hammering against the window and on the roof and on the cobblestones. From the living room I heard Kari and the guy from Bergen and later more people came and it could be that I fell asleep for a while but I woke up again, to the same rain and the same hammering and the same darkness, but also to some other sounds. And Kari started working.

At a doctor's office.

Yes, at a doctor's office.

And I came here.

Yes. How's California?

You know how California is, kid.

Yeah, but tell me anyway.

(*Silence*)

I tried to get back on my feet, sort of. Like a bird. I tried to invent hooks and backyards and walls. Places where I could live. I tried to invent windows that were not broken, windows the wind didn't blow right through. I burnt paper and boards and newspapers. I burnt diaries and pictures and it was summer. It was summer all the time, in the depths of such shivering nights.

And then Tina came, right?

Yes. She came. She said she didn't have any choice either, and her silence was as deep as a light shining.

You were a light like that too, Dad. I remember. I remember California.

Yes. And it was in such a shining light that we saw each other, Tina and I. And then we took off. To Mision Viejo. But we didn't find anything there. So we moved on to San Diego. But when we reached the city, it was dark. Eighty thousand lights switched off. A lot of night-kids, under-the-bridge kids. Skinny little girls in Converse sneakers, who trembled, who pulled down their jeans. Who thought about their souls all afternoon long.

I became a girl like that. A girl who pulled down her jeans. But first I had to grow up.

(*Silence*)

When we arrived in the city it was dark, but eventually it grew light and the heat stopped sticking so. But we found nothing there. And then we moved on to Santa Paula.

You said you wanted to go home. When you left. That's what you said.

Yes, but I was wrong. I wanted to go anywhere and call it home.

(*Silence*)

I became one of those kids, like you said. Kari went to work and came home from work. The school looked like a gigantic cat and I walked through the hallways among stuffed animals, and teachers with coffee breath who wished me welcome to Bergen and to the school. The autumn didn't come. Summer just continued. The sun was red and deep in the sky above Askøy.

Did you make friends, girlfriends?

I made friends with a girl named Theresa, an almost-neighbour who was Swedish and said Swedish words like *trädgård* and *trävligt* and who had a mother who was a feminist and who thought that all men had to get a grip because otherwise it was just no good. When autumn finally came, Theresa and I went for walks with a dog, around and around Nordnes Park for five kroner to split between the two of us, while the leaves were blown like small spaceships and the branches creaked and tumbled to the ground and the ocean was grey and wild. The wind blew and blew. Then it rained for weeks on end and everything got wet. Everything was covered with water and damp and the alleyways of Nordnes smelt of rot and cats and mildew. At the Christmas pageant, some of the boys played on tennis rackets and painted their faces like Kiss and the girls formed a chorus and mutilated a song by The Beatles and a Christmas song that I couldn't stand.

Theresa said we had to sing in the chorus simply because we were girls, next year we were going to be Kiss as well, she said, but I didn't sing, I didn't like singing and I couldn't care less about Kiss, even less about the fucking boys I said to Theresa and Theresa went quiet for the rest of the evening and it didn't help things that I was wearing a top that was way too tight, that had a laundry tag in the back on the neckline that poked and itched and Theresa said I didn't have to swear like that, that I didn't need to talk like that and be so difficult and it didn't make it any better when I said fuck off you fucking Swedish cunt and Theresa turned red as a tomato and it didn't make it any better that Kari didn't come to the Christmas pageant even though she had promised she would. Theresa pulled away from me after that, and it was just as well. But I was praised for speaking English so well.

But did you make new friends? After that?

In the beginning the girls were curious and friendly but then they decided that they didn't like me very much after all. They found all kinds of things wrong with me. I was too tall. I thought I was too pretty.

You were pretty. You were the prettiest.

Yes. I was. But I spoke the dialect from Eastern Norway and didn't know what things meant and it was so difficult explaining things to me all the time, they said. The girls. She *doesn't want to fit in*, they said.

(*Silence*)

But you made friends?

After it had been raining for 13 weeks straight, one of the teachers said that's how it is here in Bergen and I looked out at the rain and the trees, all grey, just standing all over the place. It was as if there was something waiting just around the corner. You wrote to me. You wrote that I had to come to California to visit.

Yes. And you came.

Yes. I came to California, but it was still a long time before I came. First it had to rain, first I had to overhear the girls in my class standing around in the locker room and talking about me while I was getting dressed. The night before, Kari had thrown up again and again, I had hardly slept at all and I stood there and pulled on a T-shirt and heard them talking shit about me and then I went right over and punched one of them smack in the face, it really hurt my knuckles and the girl collapsed and blood spurted out of her nose and produced a beautiful red stripe across the tiles on the wall, right below the mirror where they usually stood and dolled themselves up. The other girls bent over while they looked at me with a mixture of fear and disgust and they asked me if I was insane and I stood completely still and to the one who was staring the hardest I said, either look away or come over here, you fucking cunt. Try me.

But the boys liked you.

The boys liked me. I became that kind of girl. What was it you said?

Skinny little girls in Converse sneakers, who trembled. Who thought about their souls all afternoon long.

Yes. That kind of girl. The boys liked me. I was invited to the cinema by one who had been following me in the streets of the city centre where we went during recess. He came over to me and I looked right at him and said yes and we went and saw a film neither of us remembered afterwards, when our cold hands found each other on the steps outside the cinema, by the court house, down along the street Strandgaten, out towards Nordnes, where Kari sat in a flat without the guy from Bergen, who showed up less and less. After that the boy went home, I guess. We had kissed by Mulen, and I had run in along Strandgaten. He stood there watching me. I know. I knew it. That's why I didn't need to turn around. My lips burnt and the street, Strandgaten, looked like a gorge. Is it stupid of me to tell you this?

No. It's not stupid.

You told me many things too.

I tried, kid. It wasn't easy.

No.

I wanted to tell you everything. That was the idea. Everything that happened. I wrote you. I called. Not that often, but I wrote you. I thought I'd tell you everything that happened. Just between us witnesses, I thought. I told Tina that. She said she could hardly wait to meet you.

I liked Tina. She was weird. Once I asked her if she had ever been 16 years old and it took her a long time to answer. I liked that.

We bought bicycles. We had Grandpa Paul's money. We waited for a house in the countryside and one July morning we moved in. Tina said it was impossible to compare this joy with anything else, because you had come to visit and you walked around the house and hummed and you were reading a big fat book. The reality is us, she said and we got older and grew weary of the long days; Tina by a fireplace that didn't work and me by the doors while the birds flew, and she said things like *a hundred years with each other*.

(*Silence*)

Do you love Tina?

Yes. Yes, I do. She knew me, you know. Once she said, *hope is something one uses to measure reality*. Another time, when I was talking about Kari, she said I was the kind who liked to *label the truth*.

I didn't understand that.

No. Nobody understands it. But I understand it. I understand exactly what she means. Did that kid become your boyfriend?

No. I found Kari in her bathrobe even though it was late in the evening. For more than a year the guy from Bergen had said that the two of them were going to move in together, but for the time being they had to live apart, because first he had to straighten out some things, what they were Kari never really understood. And the days passed and the weeks passed.

And the weather changed, summer came and so on.

And the weather changed, summer came and so on. And Kari sat home alone in the evenings, all made up like a doll and the guy from Bergen came, once in a while, he rang the doorbell and then Kari lit up like a neon sign in the tiny house in Nordnes, she lit up like something old and blinking. But sometimes the guy from Bergen didn't come and Kari sat there all made up and mute and sometimes she talked to herself and love was full of snot, of tears, of nothing that helped anyway. That's how my youth began. I kissed somebody. A clumsy kiss against a green wall. I ran down the street, down Strandgaten with a boy on my lips and when I came home Kari was sitting on the couch, crying. I said she had to eat something and made cheese sandwiches and tomato soup. Kari said she couldn't take any more of this. She said: You are my dearest little girl. She said: I can never lose you, my little girl. You can never let me be all by myself, you must promise me that, Marita. Then she ate up a little of the soup before she went into the bathroom and threw it up.

(*Silence*)

That's how my youth began. She got so skinny. You stopped being thin and then Kari got thin instead. I sent pictures.

Tina hung them up here in the house.

Yeah. I remember that. She told me. Your father didn't want me to hang them up, she said. But she wanted to.

Yes, I didn't want to see Kari like that.

But that's what she became.

Yes. And it was nice of you. To think of me. Nice of you to come that summer. Tina was pleased. She cried when you left.

I liked Tina. But I didn't tell Kari. There were so many things that I never said. It went both ways. Sometimes, when she was drunk, she talked about Vera and Ann. But even then she stopped long before the morgue, long before the point where your stories began.

But my stories are just retellings.

I know. I knew that. I think we better put you to bed, Kari, I used to say. That's how my youth began. But what if the guy from Bergen comes? she said. Then I'll wake you up, I said. Do you promise? she said. I promise, I said. And one day I asked if I could borrow some of her make-up. Of course, she said, of course my

271

pearl, my beautiful little pearl. Wake me up if the guy from Bergen comes, please, she said, I have to talk to him. Do you know what we talk about? she said. I lied and said no. Sometimes we talk about you, she said. He says you are lovely and I was lovely too, just like you, in another life I was just like you are now and that was another time and we took the America Line and Ylva wasn't the asshole she's become now and everything was light. And then she asked: Do you feel lightness? Is there lightness where you are, Marita?

Did you hear all of the sounds?

Yes. All of them. And the rain. And the sounds from the living room when the guy from Bergen came. Sobbing or whatever it was, and Kari breaking some furniture.

But what about your youth?

My youth was of glass. I learnt that later, from Andreas. He taught me the word *glass*. He said: *Adolescence is made of glass*. He was totally obsessed with it. With me. Adolescence sings perfectly, he said, but that was later. Before that I had black circles around my eyes. The boys in my class said I looked like a panda bear. But then I started wearing skirts so short that the boys didn't say a word and the male teachers didn't say a word, but the lady teacher we had for math said she had to send me to the principal who was a woman, who for an eternity talked about decency and about the kind of signals one sent out into the world. She said she understood that it was difficult, that adolescence was difficult and I said *abyss* and the lady principal said what is an abyss and I said *the lightness*. The next time the boy asked if I wanted to go to the cinema I said no and when he asked me why, I said: Get lost.

(*Silence*)

It will be light soon.

Here, too. Is this how we speak to each other?

This is how we speak to each other. You grow and grow. You are the only one who is you.

I remember you said that. I wrote it in my diary. At night I heard ravens outside my bedroom window, I heard the footsteps of the old lady in the flat above us. Kari went to work and came home from work and one day she stopped going to work altogether.

What did you say about me?

Dad is in America, I said if somebody asked, and then I didn't say any more about it.

It will be light soon.

Yes. Here too. It gets dark and then it gets light.

You had the shortest skirt in the city.

Yes. And knee socks and basketball sneakers. I was friends with the boys. I pulled down my skirt and lied

273

about New York. I dyed my hair black and made up my enormous eyes and sometimes the boys and I went up to Nygård Park in the evenings and we sat under a tree and afterwards I wiped their adolescent sperm off my fingers, wiped my fingers on the grass while the boys buttoned up their trousers and I lied or told truths about New York, because nobody had heard of New Jersey, nobody knew about Vera or Ann or—later, when I came back from California—about how it felt to stand beneath a sun as big as an orange and the smell of the ocean and the smell of the sand and your increasingly dry tears, Dad, your increasingly grey heart, and that was home in a way, your heart writing me letters a couple of times a year, calling me kid, calling me my little girl and once: My little girls.